The Expenda

Patrick Mackeown

Season's greetings
Patrick Mackeown

Also by Patrick Mackeown:

The Cardinal's Blood
Midwinter's Children

The Expendability Doctrine

Patrick Mackeown

BookScape

First published 2006 by BookScape

This edition published 2006 by BookScape
PO Box 53225 London N3 2XW
www.bookscape.co.uk

ISBN 978-0-9554328-0-4
ISBN 0-9554328-0-4

1 3 5 7 9 8 6 4 2

A CIP catalogue record for this book is available
from the British Library.

Cover design: Lorraine Castle, Vibration Media
Cover foreground photo: © Rob Fox
Cover background photo: © Loretta Hostettler
Cover typeface: © Jakob Fischer

The Expendability Doctrine is also available in eBook format:
ISBN 978-0-9554328-1-1 (Adobe Reader)
ISBN 978-0-9554328-2-8 (Mobipocket)

CHAPTER 1

Hilary Connors was surprised by just how easy killing somebody could be; like everything else in life, you just had to put your mind to it. She crossed a disused railway line tugging her cream-coloured, baby alpaca coat about her ankles. An East-Anglian sea breeze stung her face. She huddled, pulling her chinchilla collar close around her neck and blew into her hands. She couldn't feel her toes. Suddenly, there he was. He didn't look all that bad for a murderer, perhaps a bit slim, but he had a nice smile.

'You startled me,' she said.

'Force of habit,' he replied. 'People never hear me coming. I wouldn't live long if they did. Now, can we get on with it?'

'Right, yes, sorry,' she said blushing. 'What do you want me to do?'

'First the money: Five thousand now. You got it with you?'

She nodded.

'Then ten thousand: You wait till I contact you. Then a further five thousand. You never contact me, you can't. You pay what I say, how I say, when I say. Nothing happens till I get the money. Got any problems with that?'

She shook her head.

'Never be late. Don't even think about being late or missing a payment. If you make that mistake, you'll never make another. Are we understanding each other?'

She nodded.

'Photograph?'

She pulled the torn wedding photograph from her handbag. He smiled again, running his fingers down the jagged edge of the fragmented image.

'I like that,' he said nodding. 'Have you got a whole photo?'

She shook her head, 'it's the only one. I burned the others, all of them. I burned everything.'

'Where's the other half?'

'I don't know, I threw it away, I think.'

'Where?'

'I don't know, I don't know!'

'OK,' he said softly, 'it's OK.'

They sat for a minute in silence.

'You OK?'

She sniffed, 'yeah, never better.' She wiped her eyes with her wrist. After a few minutes she asked, 'what do I do now?'

'You go home and wait. You'll never see me again. Have you told anyone else about this?'

She shook her head.

'You're sure? No-one at all? Think carefully before you answer. If I have to come back and clean up after your mistakes, it'll mean killing everybody. Do you understand what I'm saying? I don't just mean him. I mean you and whoever it is you told about this.'

Hilary didn't respond. The gunman raised his voice slightly to jog her back to the matter in hand.

'You understand me, Mrs Connors?'

'Yes,' she whispered, 'yes, I understand, I told no-one, absolutely no-one.'

'If I hear my name mentioned anywhere, I'll know it came from you, do you understand what that means?'

She nodded.

'That's it then,' he said.

Hilary walked unsteadily back to her bicycle. She was determined not to look behind her, fearing that it might not be safe. For reasons she couldn't clarify, looking back towards a killer as he prepared his future strike felt more dangerous than sitting beside him while he studied her torn photograph of his next victim.

She hadn't realised how difficult it was to cycle, wearing a full-length coat. It hadn't been a problem earlier, nothing had. She had been concentrating so hard on not being terrified, that she hadn't noticed the journey at all. Every time she bent down to gather up the hem of her coat, her bicycle wobbled frantically. She longed to be at the wheel of her car.

All the silent roads and empty shopping centre car parks made her ache with desire for the return of normality. The recent sharp petrol price increases had driven many local shopkeepers out of businesses. People were going hungry. The local television news reports brought their stories to her attention before she could change the channel. All over the country petrol stations had run out of fuel. Hilary and all her friends had been reduced to cycling. She didn't really care whether petrol prices came down or not, just as long as she could drive her car and buy clothes.

As she veered towards the brightly lit windows of Liberty, the most expensive store on her route, her right, high-heeled shoe fell off. Breaking, turning and dismounting with only one shoe was difficult. Hilary hated bicycles.

Now her house was almost within walking distance. She dismounted and pushed the bicycle along the eerily deserted street.

In the driveway of her modern, detached house she ran her palm gently over the hood of her convertible Mercedes. She let the bicycle fall into her flowerbed and entered the house. Then, gathering her cat into her arms, Hilary sank into her sofa. She tipped the dregs from a heavy, dimpled-based whiskey tumbler into her kitchen sink, but did not bother to wash the glass. Her house had ice, but she was without the will-power to walk a few feet to her fridge. She measured two fingers into the glass and poured another healthy splash on top for good measure. The first two fingers of gin she knocked back with a single swig. She also measured her next two large mouthfuls. Beyond that, there seemed no point in measuring. The following morning she would have no recollection of drinking from the neck of the bottle. Eventually, when the time came to wake up, she would stagger towards the television, knocking letters and magazines from her occasional table onto the floor with the hem of her coat just as she had the morning before and the one before that. She was a terrible wreck and she knew it. Soon though, for that day at least, she'd be beyond caring.

She switched on her television. Suddenly a terrible fear gripped her. Perhaps she had been seen. Perhaps someone knew that she'd met with a murderer and reported her to the police. Hilary knew such fears were irrational. She knew perfectly well that no-one had seen her. The streets of her town were completely deserted. She drank more alcohol. Her hands were shaking. She turned on the news and tried to focus on her television screen.

CHAPTER 2

In the news report which Hilary forced herself to follow, a full picture of the developing international petroleum crisis emerged. Every single one of Great Britain's streets was deserted. The same was true in every European capital. Cars were silent. And it was clear even to Hilary, whose head swirled as she glugged her way into alcoholic oblivion, that all was not well either in the world of television news. She tried still harder to blot-out her plan of Keith's murder, but regardless of how much she drank the crime wouldn't leave her thoughts.

'We'll bring you this report in a second,' a BBC news woman read out. 'Please be patient.'

Hilary's television screen showed an image of Number Ten Downing Street's famous black front door. It was closed. She waited.

'Here comes the prime minister,' the newsreader announced. 'The government has been in crisis talks all morning. We understand that there are food shortages in several towns and cities. We'll have a statement about law and order, in a moment, from Britain's most senior police officer, but now we go live to the prime minister.'

The leader of Britain's government still did not appear.

'We have more breaking news for you,' the woman in the studio explained as she shuffled sheets of paper and dropped them onto the floor. 'Crude oil prices on the world markets have just risen again for the third time in two days. The situation in the Middle East has now deteriorated even further, and we expect it to get still worse. More fighting has broken out after an unknown number of gunmen opened fire on a convoy of buses travelling to the Israeli enclave of Hebron on the West Bank, inside one of the fledgling Palestinian controlled 'autonomous areas'. Israel, in response to the third terrorist attack in two weeks, conducted a lightning strike against government offices in Syria. No deaths have been reported. Yesterday, the Israeli prime minister accused the Syrian government of supporting terrorist activities. Tony Leadbrook reports.'

There was a silence for several minutes as the reporter scrambled for the Leadbrook recording.

The BBC's international correspondent began, 'analysts widely predict that the United States, already overstretched in Iraq and resented by the Arab world, will exacerbate the situation by supporting the Israeli strikes. The Arabic oil exporters have begun restricting production and raising prices still further. OPEC has given an ultimatum to America; the United States must either stop supporting Israeli massacres, and militarised aggression, or face a complete suspension of oil sales. These are the scenes all over America as panic buying spreads across the country.'

From an American news crew helicopter a cameraman scanned endless queues of cars, baking in the midday sun. People could be seen clearly, fighting on garage forecourts below. The report then showed oil prices on the New York Stock Exchange rising steadily every second. The usually frantic market traders wiped sweat from their faces as they waved their arms and shouted. One market maker in the centre of the camera shot shrugged his shoulders and poured water on his face. He was pushed aside by paramedics as they pulled an exchange floor manager from his office on a stretcher. As the lead paramedic shouted, 'bring me the cardiac defibrillator', the stretcher crashed into the television crew. For a second the view of the exchange floor was inverted, until a trader stood on the camera. For an instant Hilary's television screen went blank as the recording from America was cut off.

The London based BBC news reader continued, 'as we wait to bring you live coverage of the prime minister's address, let's go to our reporter Lesley Anderson for more news on the momentous events at home.'

By now the BBC newsreader had no papers in front of her at all. She clearly did not know what to say next and nobody was helping her.

'I can tell you that the government will not add more taxes onto petrol prices,' she announced, as if she'd just remembered an entirely unconnected fact. As she spoke the door to Number Ten opened and the prime minister walked out briskly into the centre of the road. He looked calm, almost cheerful. For at least two seconds he smiled. Despite herself, Hilary smiled too. And then the government leader began to speak.

'We have made the necessary emergency order in council. I have made absolutely certain that everybody understands we must all do more to improve the fuel situation. I have spoken to the Saudi government and they have assured me that they are seeking to reach a settlement. But there is more we can do here at home.' As he turned to re-enter his official residence, the BBC correspondent called out, 'Prime Minister, isn't it true that the whole world is being held hostage by OPEC? What are the alternatives? Why don't we get Siberian oil supplies from Russia instead?'

'Rest assured, that everything that can be done is being done,' was the curt reply he received, before the British premier disappeared.

CHAPTER 3

In another corner of the same town, Hilary's husband Keith Connors was preparing to go to work without his car. Travelling without a car was something he'd not done for years because Keith detested all forms of physical exercise. He loathed cycling, but he hated walking even more. And yet still more than either of these cruel and unusual punishments, he hated being exposed to the rain. The weather report had informed him that rain was inevitable and because of this, he was in a hideous mood. Keith was wealthy, much more so than almost everyone he knew. But today the one simple thing he wanted most, a ride to work, eluded even him. He cursed aloud.

As the oil-rich businessman crossed his Chinese granite paving and ducked under his garden's Portland stone arch, he got none of his usual satisfaction from his precious possessions. On either side of the arch, statues of Athena and Apollo stood watching over a marble, ornamental carp pool. Today none of his exquisite things pleased him. He wrenched open the door of his nineteenth century coach house and swore as he fumbled for the light switch. Reaching his bicycle was no easy task. Clambering between his Bentley and his Aston Martin Keith found the bicycle that he hated so much. Four revolutions along the cobble stones of Saint Anne's Terrace, outside his house, were enough to alert him to the fact that both of his tyres were completely flat. He stomped home and threw the cycle down in disgust. But try as he might, he could not find a bicycle pump. After more than half an hour of frantic searching and imaginative cursing, Keith Connors set off for Andall Guildhall on foot.

Despite the fact that it was already after ten o'clock on a weekday, most of the shops along his route were closed. All around him piles of rubbish spilled their contents, which blew across the street. Slightly ahead of him, a large, dark rat twisted awkwardly to lick a vivid scar on its shoulder. The filthy animal's wound, he could see, was surrounded by a balding, moulting patch of mange. As he approached, the enormous rodent bared its yellow fangs, before pelting into a nearby alley. As he glanced briefly, in the direction of the town's commercial docks, he caught a glimpse of two scantily

13

clad young women scurrying through the eerily deserted Andall streets. He pulled his coat closer around his shoulders and hurried on. A long, untidy police barricade blocked off the leafy residential areas of Princess Street, Saint Anne's and Regent Street, in the direction from which he had come. On the other side, ahead of the barricade, lay open waste ground which had once been covered with factories. And beyond that, the sprawl of nineteen sixties concrete high-rises. Beside and beyond those lay the failed social housing projects, which made up the Marchant Estates. It was here that having money really made a difference. Wealthy people like Keith who could afford the houses at the top of the hill had a police guard to protect their lives and property if the crisis worsened still further. Less fortunate people in the same town got no such protection. Repeated pleas to erect more barricades between the less privileged private houses on Keith's hill and the Marchant had been turned down. Connors was grateful for their manned security division. He and his neighbours took it in turns to bring the policemen tea. Some even brought sandwiches and cakes.

He felt better now. Once again he felt able to appreciate how much better off he was than so many of his neighbours. His smile returned. He even paused at the charcoal brazier to chat with the two constables on duty. The younger one, who was stamping his feet and blowing into his hands, Keith guessed, was still a probationer. Connors suspected that the poor lad was longing for his word processor and the banter of the office, instead of his duty protecting these cold and empty streets.

Finally, at the end of his journey, Keith Connors pressed his face against the windows at the rear of Andall Guildhall. He'd not heard from his friend, Doctor Simmons, who organised the Andall Chamber of Commerce's special events. Instead, all he had was a notification telling him that other arrangements were being made and the guildhall would be open. The hall itself looked deserted. Keith tried to enter doors at the front and back. He failed. As he turned to leave, a voice called out to him from the hall's middle door.

'You, there! Hello. Come to Doctor Simmons' meeting on exporting from Colombia?'

'I'd assumed that there wouldn't be anybody here,' Keith admitted in surprise. 'It's been quieter here in the last few months than it was in the centre of Alaska all last winter.'

'You look frozen to death,' Keith's host exclaimed, escorting the businessman into the hall through a side entrance. 'Follow me. I'll get a couple of Scotches to warm us up.'

Keith and the stranger meandered towards the guildhall bar. They sipped their whiskeys slowly, in front of an open fire.

'I suppose we're the only ones here,' Keith mused, looking at his watch.

Just as his host was about to answer, a burley, red-faced American, wearing a double-breasted suit and orange running shoes, bounded over to meet them.

'Hi ya'll, don't get up,' he boomed, shook hands with Connors' companion and introduced himself to Keith.

'The whole world looks like it's gone to hell in a hand basket, doesn't it? There ain't no time like the present. What'd'ya say we get started without the others?'

They moved into a conference room, which was set for thirty people.

'So, Keith, Dick here tells me you Brits are willing to make sacrifices to help the US economy out of a hell-uva-hole. What'd'ya say? How would you like to work for me, get these economies back up on their feet? I'm not just talking about the US economy here. I'm talking about the British economy, too. How would you like to get them back up and running, make a fortune in the process and get yourself made into a hero all at the same time? Dick said we'd have a lot of people here. I see you were expecting quite a few folks. But I guess they couldn't make it, huh? I guess nobody can travel in this British country of yours because you all ain't got no gasoline neither. We gotta do somethin' about that right now! Keith, I'm tellin ya. What'd'ya say? You Brits are great folks, you know? You know we got a lot in common?'

The Texan put a meaty arm around Keith's shoulders. Keith could see that this was a man who clearly enjoyed giving theatrical performances. This room was almost entirely empty. And yet here he was gesturing and lecturing as if the whole world was waiting for his every last word.

'I'll tell you what,' the burly Texan continued, hardly pausing for breath. 'Since ya'll are the only ones over here, why don't we all carve up my billion dollar oil exploration contracts between the three of us right here in this room, right now?'

Keith was surprised. He always expected to make money. It was his forte, but even for him this deal was proving to be an exceptionally easy one to make. He ignored a powerful instinct which told him that nothing ever proved this easy. He'd never seen anybody offer him, or anyone else, billions of dollars before. Things like that just didn't happen. But then, he conceded, these were exceptional times.

His English companion had leaned forward towards the American. Keith was keen not to appear reticent.

'Explain,' he called out to the Texan. 'What was it that you had in mind?'

CHAPTER 4

As Keith sat in the warm guildhall discussing oil contracts which could make him even richer than he already was, another man waited nearby to kill him. The assassin, who Hilary Connors had hired to murder her husband, had no name. More precisely, he had twelve names, but he hadn't a single name which could be considered an identifier. Despite that failing, though, he did well enough without one. Having no name didn't prevent him from spying on Keith's luxury house from the wildlife hide on the Orwell estuary. Nor did it prevent him conducting forays into the successful businessman's splendid garden. He'd never left a single thing to chance in any of his previous murders. This killing would be no different.

As he planted a tiny, convex speaker below Connors' kitchen window, he imagined the enraged businessman erupting from his house. Hilary Connors, though comical on a bicycle, had been accurate in every detail about her soon-to-be ex-husband's habits. The assassin and his murderous client were agreed that a recording of fighting tom cats, threatening his ornamental carp, would bring Keith Connors rushing to his death. The assassin checked his nine millimetre automatic pistol for the third time in twenty minutes. The silencer was tight, he already knew that, but he checked it again, anyway. Then he measured the distance to the hide. It was exactly six hundred and seventy paces and it took him only seconds to reach it from the middle of the garden. He re-paced the distance between the statue and the Koki carp pool. It was eleven feet. He knew the distance, nevertheless, he re-paced it twice more.

The three businessmen waited patiently for Keith Connors' legal representatives to settle themselves. His lawyer, Brian Cardman, a balding man in his late fifties, was sweating heavily.

'I'm sorry, I'm so sorry,' Cardman stammered, shaking his jacket. 'I haven't walked that far in years.'

'Ya'll want to maybes take five?' the Texan suggested helpfully.

'I beg your pardon?' the solicitor gasped, 'take five what?'

'Ya'll know Britain's Trade Minister Lord Uxbridge will be visiting Tripoli next month? He's taking on over a trade delegation which includes me. And, ya'll wanna come on over there?' the Texan continued, scouring the room as though the twenty eight absentees had miraculously appeared.

'The British all have arranged several meetings with Libya's National Oil Company. They all even persuaded Libya to amend her gas laws. Twenty of the largest US oil companies all had assets over in Libya frozen in the Eighties when they all were forced to head on out of the country by President Ronald Reagan. Those assets still are held in trust. Our new president asked me to locate British companies to pump oil at US sites. US companies still can't do business with Libya, by law. We've got to obey the trade sanctions. Americans can't drill Libyan oil without a new bill in Congress. But you British guys can. With your help we can get up and running as soon as. The machinery is all there, ready and waiting to go. I've got the plans right here. You can take them straight to your British employers. It's all been done for you. Everything has been worked out by the US. We'll even give you a percentage. Because all the others couldn't make it, you get their share, too. It's what we call, in the US, a no-brainer. See, look here.'

The Texan opened his case to reveal an enormous pile of papers, contracts and charts. Some hours, a number of whiskeys and several presentations later, they had examined and copied more than eleven contracts, totalling three and a half billion dollars each. Weighed down with documents Keith Connors and his solicitor parted on the guildhall steps. He waved to the remaining men in the brightly lit room, as he began his chilly walk home.

At a quarter to nine that evening, the assassin watched Connors switch on the hall light. He moved into the adjoining room and deposited a bundle of papers. Loosening his necktie, Connors opened a mahogany cabinet door and poured himself a large whiskey. In anticipation, the waiting man released the safety catch on his automatic pistol. He watched Keith move into the drawing room. As he approached the window to draw the curtains Connors glanced straight into the eyes of his killer. Then, abruptly, drawing the curtains almost together, he returned to his upholstered armchair. The hunter waited for at least a minute, but no other figures moved inside the house. From his hiding place, he listened to the sound of a man's voice. He had to be sure his victim was alone. He crept forward, feeling the path ahead of him. Now he crouched, a fraction beneath the drawing room windowsill. The room was completely empty. A single glass stood on the Chippendale occasional table in the centre of the room. It could be a sign that Connors was alone. He waited. Connors returned to the centre of the room, holding a telephone to his ear. He approached the window for a second time, closing the curtains completely. It was confirmed then, he was indeed alone.

The assassin felt his way behind the statue and began to play the recording. Even from where he lay, at the foot of the fish pond, he couldn't hear the recording himself, but he knew his victim was receiving its full benefit. Within seconds, as he had planned, an angry man rushed from the kitchen doorway.

Keith was panting by the time he reached the marble pool. Cursing fluently, he thrashed about for a minute. And then suddenly he stood completely still. Though he didn't understand why, he felt the presence of someone behind him. He had almost managed to turn round, when a surprising force sent him crashing into the water. The killer sprinted from his cover. He felt Keith's pulse quickly and retrieved the speaker. Within seconds he had scaled the covered water butt, rolled across the lowest end of the coach house roof and jumped onto the cobbled street below. Without losing a moment he sprinted beneath a tree. Nothing moved. He set off again. As swiftly and silently as a fox he slipped away into the darkness.

CHAPTER 5

Hilary awoke downstairs in her sitting room. She was wearing her dressing gown, but did not remember taking her clothes off. In fact, she couldn't remember anything from the day before at all. Her mouth was fuzzy and her head ached. She stumbled towards her telephone answering machine and played a recorded message from her son, Luke. The boy seemed to be saying *'Got two dads'*. Hilary assumed that it was supposed to be funny. Her son Luke's odd humour troubled her and she blamed his father for it. But then, she blamed the boy's father for almost everything.

At that moment her doorbell rang. Hilary's temples throbbed as she fumbled towards the glass panel in the centre of her front door. Behind it, outside, Hilary could make out two distinct figures.

'Yes, what do you want?' she asked, unsteadily, through her intercom, as she took an enormous swig of alcohol from her glass. Drinking in the morning cleared her head and stopped her hands from shaking.

A man's voice replied faintly, 'Mrs Connors, Mrs Hilary Connors, could you open the door, please? It's the police. We need to talk to you.'

Hilary opened the door as far as her security chain would allow. Two warrant cards presented themselves directly in her line of sight.

One visitor was plainly a detective because he had no uniform. For an instant that fact did not register with Hilary at all. She was still not thinking clearly. The plain-clothed officer was a tall, black man in his thirties. He didn't look official in his green cotton trousers and roll-necked jumper, instead he looked kind. Hilary smiled and then winced as her headache pulsed. Behind the detective, a younger, uniformed woman stood.

'My name is Hawthorne,' the black policeman said. 'Detective Inspector Hawthorne. Perhaps we ought to sit down. There's no easy way to say this, I'm afraid I've got bad news.'

Hilary started to panic. Her muddled head had still not fully grasped the situation. She now understood her son's telephone message. It said: *'Gone to Dad's'*. It was not a joke. His message was real. The boy had gone to visit his father! And Hilary's hired assassin had gone there, too. Of course her son Luke had no way of knowing the kind of danger he was in. How could he know? Only she knew.

The frightened mother stood blinking in front of her guests. She couldn't feel her legs. They had simply stopped working. Her jittering right knee caused the liquid in her glass to splatter.

Hawthorne cleared his throat,

'Mrs Connors...' He stopped.

Hilary's knees were bending.

'Oh God, oh no, oh my God no!' she wailed, covering her mouth with her free hand.

The detective continued, 'I'm very sorry to have to tell you this, Mrs Connors, it's your husband...'

Inspector Hawthorne tried to catch Hilary's whiskey glass as it dropped from her hand. The trio froze for a split second as the tumbler spun through the air. Then Hilary collapsed. The police officers arranged the unconscious woman on the sofa. Her gown fell open revealing her nakedness. From her right hip all the way up to the breast on the same side Hilary Connors had a vivid scar. The woman police officer leaned forward and pulled their hostess' gown tight around her body.

'How bad is the scarring on her body?' Hawthorne asked.

'It's extensive, sir,' the uniformed woman, Constable Anderson, explained. 'It goes around her ribs right into the centre of her back.'

The detective pinched his lips together.

'I wonder what could have done so much damage,' he said. 'A car accident maybe? How is she?'

'She's fine, sir. Would you like me to stay with her for a while?' Anderson offered.

'Hilary and her husband lived apart but they still kept the same doctor,' Hawthorne mused. 'I need to ask him about her scars. Will you be alright if I leave you here?' he called to Anderson from Hilary's front door.

Before Anderson could reply the inspector had gone. The detective already knew who Hilary Connors' doctor was. He and the doctor had already spoken about the dead man, Hilary's husband. At that time the policeman had no plans to visit the physician. A phone call had been adequate. Now things were different.

21

He walked briskly. The air was cold. There were two ways to get to Dr Adams' house from Hilary's estate. The first, though longer, avoided the high-rise housing estates which many Andall residents so disliked and feared. In broad daylight he should have been able to walk through them safely enough. That was his problem. His police force was as short of petrol as the rest of the country's population. If he got attacked in the Marchant housing estate, would anyone from his police force arrive in time to rescue him?

The first tower block, Mandela House, which stood at the eastmost edge of the estate, was now only a few hundred yards ahead of him. He had to make his mind up. Would he go in or would he go round?

The detective passed the first high-rise block. Decay lay all around him. On the ground floor of Mandela House, two flats had been boarded up by the local council. The boards had been partially removed. The whole place reeked of stale urine. It was a perfect drug dealing den. Hawthorne hurried past. He had eleven other blocks of flats to pass before he reached open ground again. It still made sense for him to turn back.

It occurred to him how ridiculous it was that he, an experienced police officer, should fear the walk though a residential area of his own town in the middle of the day. But that was a fact. Serious assaults on the Marchant Estate were so common that most of them went unrecorded. Now it worried him that he might be undertaking the journey to prove to himself that he could. Was he doing that, or was he saving precious time? He'd passed the third housing block now. Soon he'd have as far to go in either direction. Two boys crossed the street in front of him. Both were in their early teens. Their faces were covered by sporty hoods. More youths appeared. They were all carrying sticks. There were now several boys on either side of him.

'Who are ye?' one boy said. Hawthorne carried on walking.

'Who the fuck are ye?' the boy repeated. And then added, 'I hate fucking coons!' The detective was now halfway across the estate. He was surrounded, and things had started to get unpleasant. There was nothing he could do now except walk and hope.

CHAPTER 6

Luke Connors, Hilary's son, was a hard-working student and a promising sportsman. At his university in the North of England, daily life had become disorganised by the international petrol crisis. He had already made four attempts to hand in his winter term paper and on every occasion he had failed. At Macarthy University the teaching staff and almost all the students had simply disappeared. The halls were empty. Luke was alone.

He did not come from a close-knit family. He had not seen his mother for more than a year. His choice now was to remain in an empty university where he might run out of food or return to his girl-friend Monique, in Andall, on the other side of the country. After some indecision, Luke decided to return home. In spite of the fuel strike, the travel method he chose was hitch-hiking. On almost deserted roads it was difficult, but two women picked him up.

And so he arrived before noon, in a heavy downpour at a transport cafe on the outskirts of the city of Nottingham. The neighbourhood was chaotic. Due to the petrol shortages lorries could not travel. They simply parked on both sides of the road in front of the cafe. Stationary heavy goods vehicles crammed together nose to tail, sometimes three deep. Luke ran for shelter from the rain and his mobile phone rang. The voice was his mother's. Her recorded message was confusing.

'Don't go to Keith's. Luke, are you alright?' she said. 'Tell me you're alright. Oh God, Luke, please tell me you're alright!'

Of course he was alright. He didn't know what she meant. He had more than two hundred miles to walk to reach the south east coast of England, but he was fine. The student put his phone back into his rucksack and pressed on.

On several occasions he stayed with complete strangers. Never once was he asked his business, save but to establish that he was hungry and tired and had a long way to travel. The whole country seemed conscious of the fact that everybody had a duty to help anybody in need. At first the student found it strange that people he didn't know offered him food when he could see plainly that they didn't have enough to feed themselves. He was too hungry to refuse them. But he kept a list of the people to whom he was indebted. It was a long list.

Luke Connors entered his parents' home town by crossing a railway bridge on Andall's northernmost tip. He knew that his mother was not at her house, because he'd telephoned there earlier. And, since his father didn't much mind what he did, he'd decided to use Keith's house as a temporary base, at least until he'd established the lie of the land. Whilst his own father was an undeniably unemotional character, at least he wasn't a psychopath. His girlfriend's father was, on the other hand. And so her house was out of the question.

He arrived exhausted and famished at the barricade at the bottom of Regent Street, a few hundred meters from his father's front door. He was met by a uniformed policeman who spoke to him nicely.

'Now then, lad, where are you heading?' the constable asked with a smile.

'Number One, Saint Anne's Terrace. Can I come through?' the student replied.

The policeman's demeanour changed instantly.

'Number One, you say? What business have you there then?' the constable replied, reaching for his notepad.

'I live there,' the student asserted, tensing. His voice had risen at least an octave. He was defending himself, without knowing why.

'Then we need to talk to you,' the constable explained, 'follow me.'

Luke followed the police officer across the wasteland which separated the desirable residential area where his father lived from the shops and businesses of downtown Andall. Presently they drew up in front of a rather ugly, red-brick building which advertised itself as the local police station.

Inside Luke Connors met Simon Hawthorne. The student had never seen a black detective before. If he was surprised he was too exhausted to show it. The detective smiled as he extended his hand towards the bedraggled undergraduate.

'I'd say welcome, but it's not much of a welcome, is it?' Hawthorne said.

The boy looked done in. He hardly looked fit to hear what Hawthorne had to say. But he had to be told regardless. Hawthorne hadn't had much experience of telling people that their loved-ones had died. It was the worst conceivable task that any officer ever

24

faced. Of course Detective Inspector Hawthorne was acutely aware that however unpleasant his current task might be for him, for Luke Connors it would be infinitely worse.

'I don't suppose you've had anything to eat, have you?' the inspector asked, pausing to watch Luke's reaction.

Anticipation of hot food lifted the young man's spirits. His face lit up. As Hawthorne mulled over the unpleasant announcement that he was about to deliver, he led the way to his police station's canteen.

'You must have been on your way to your father's house?' the detective began, pulling out a chair across the table from where Luke sat.

The younger man nodded.

'How does bangers and mash sound?' the policeman added, making an effort to sound casual.

'Sounds good,' Luke replied, not taking his eyes from the rim of a polystyrene cup of tea a uniformed officer had given him. The food arrived and the young man shovelled it into his face as Hawthorne sat and watched.

'Why have you brought me here?' the student asked, wiping gravy from his chin at the same time. Hawthorne paused. Luke stopped eating and looked up. The fearful feeling he'd had earlier, outside his father's house, was returning. The detective's face was still friendly but the laughter lines from around his eyes had gone.

'It's about your father,' the inspector explained. 'I'm sorry to have to tell you this, I'm afraid he's dead. We're not sure exactly what happened yet. That's why we need to talk to everyone, including you. It's a terrible shock, I'm sorry. I have to ask you some questions, though.'

'How,' Luke's voice crackled and failed. 'I mean how? What happened?'

'Do you know of anyone who might want to harm your father?' Hawthorne probed.

'No,' Luke admitted.

'Where will you stay tonight?' the inspector continued. 'You can't go to Saint Anne's Terrace. It's a crime scene. Have you spoken to your mother?'

'I tried to reach her twice but there was no response,' Luke explained. Perhaps I should go to her house.' Hawthorne nodded and stood up.

'I'll go with you,' he said.

Almost an hour later, the student and the inspector turned into the short, asphalt drive at the entrance to Hilary Connors' house. Hawthorne rang the bell and waited. When nothing happened he pressed his face against Hilary's kitchen window.

'Find a way inside and then let me in,' Hawthorne instructed. Luke complied. It took the duo no more than a few seconds to confirm that Hilary's house was empty.

'Where does she keep her passport?' the detective snapped.

They found no sign of Hilary Connors and no sign of her passport.

CHAPTER 7

In the early afternoon of the day following her husband's murder, Hilary Connors made her escape. She had been waiting almost an hour when a light helicopter landed in the centre of Andall High School playing field. The deafened fugitive from British justice cowered with an index finger jammed inside each ear. Her rescuer and co-conspirator, a round-bodied, ruddy-faced, Texan hopped to the ground on the far side of his aircraft. His curly, fair hair blew about him in all directions as he approached.

'How ya'll doin', OK?' he shouted over the helicopter's engine noise.

As Hilary climbed into the craft's worn, leather passenger seat she noticed how small its glass cockpit was. She felt exposed and vulnerable. Next to strike her was the machine's complex array of controls, dials, switches and gauges. She smiled nervously as the pilot strapped himself in. And more to herself than her companion she muttered, 'is this thing really going to fly?'

Her host smiled reassuringly, as his tiny vessel pitched forward and scooped itself along the ground. The terrified passenger gripped her seat with both hands as they skimmed, ever faster, across the remaining gap between the centre of the field and the boundary hedge. Flinching as she anticipated the impact of the hedgerow in her face, Hilary closed her eyes. Later, braving a quick look past her feet, she marvelled at the sight of the ground down below. I'm just sitting here on this invisible cushion of air, she thought. Her host leaned over and pointed at the town disappearing rapidly beneath them.

'When ya'll get on out,' he advised loudly, 'make sure ya'll walk ahead on towards the front of the helicopter. Else the rotor on the back is gonna catch ya'll out.'

When he banked sharply over Andall town's high church steeple she had both a sudden and complete sensation of swooping. Without relaxing at all, Hilary leaned back to listen to the rotor blades chopping through the air above her head. They were approaching Dover. By the time the dazzling, white, chalk cliffs gleamed beneath them and they passed out over the English Channel, Hilary Connors had begun to settle down. Now she was free. For her, crossing the Kent coastline marked her point of no return. Had she been thinking clearly, she would have realised that point had passed long ago.

As their tiny vehicle skipped and skimmed across the waves, Hilary plucked up enough courage to voice a feeble protest, 'aren't we flying a little low?' She began gripping the seat edges again. And then she ventured, 'why do we keep dipping like that?'

Over the sound of his rotor blades the American explained, 'ya'll confuse the British radar system. They all got several well known errors. Ya'll call it sneaking on in under the radar horizon.'

Much as the chalk cliffs of Kent had flashed beneath them earlier, so too did their French cousins on the opposite shore. Within minutes of reaching foreign territory the pilot began his descent. Hilary closed her eyes for a second time as the ground careered towards her. She sighed as the light aircraft plopped onto the ground. As her companion wound the rotors down, she unclipped her seatbelt and opened her eyes. Her Normandy farmhouse looked more inviting than it had when she'd last seen it. It was now a refuge. Its downstairs windows were open and the door propped wide with a chair. But there was no time for rest. Work needed to be done.

'Ya'll wanna run on inside an' check everything's in order?' the American advised in a forthright manner. It wasn't a suggestion. It was an instruction. He began passing her case through the passenger door and pointing towards the house.

'Come on now,' he added. 'Time's wastin'.'

Hilary nodded and with her head bowed in an instinctive manner, she trotted out of the aircraft's downdraft. The inside of her house was cool. She splashed her face with cold water and waved to her companion. It didn't take her long to check the main part of the house; her tiny study was just as she'd left it. She flicked the dial on her safe impatiently, and ruffled through her papers. It seemed unnecessary to be taking these precautions, but the pilot had asked for them, and she had no real objections. Everything was perfectly in order. She was sure of that. On her way back to the front door she checked the freezer compartment for ice cubes. There were none. Her sense of perfection was dented, but not irreparably. She poured a measure of gin into an earthenware mug and sipped it slowly as she crossed the field.

'Ya'll checked on everything?' her companion called from his aircraft window, as she approached. She nodded, reaching up to lower his window from outside.

'Be ready for when we all head on out to North Africa,' he cautioned. 'Ya'll wanna be the first to see the new oil company. Don't be holdin' us up now. D'ya hear?'

She nodded. She knew his plans and had no intention of spoiling them.

The pilot spun-up the rotors and climbed into the sky. Hilary Connors turned her back on the noisy machine and began to prepare her belongings. She had no time to rest. The visit to her French home had only been planned as the first step in her escape sequence. Anyone trying to find her would need to know which country she was in, and, with the exception of her present companion, no-one did. She was determined to make tracing herself as difficult as possible. It was unfair on her only son. She knew that. But knowing that his mother was alive, and rotting in a British gaol, instead, wouldn't have been any fairer upon him either. She knew that all of her options were unpalatable. But some were also profitable. And profit joined liberty at the top of Hilary's list of objectives. With those ends in mind, Hilary Connors, with a different name, would soon be boarding an ordinary commercial flight to Libya.

CHAPTER 8

In the arrivals hall at Tripoli International Airport, Hilary Connors queued with the other perspiring westerners from her flight. Their airplane had been the first to touch down there for some time. Her greeting was exactly the same as everybody else's. Everything in her shoulder bag was tipped and shaken onto the stationary conveyor belt in front of them. She watched, with a growing sense of unease as her toiletries and underwear were scattered, studied and scraped into an untidy pile. As she looked on, her envelopes and letters were opened and read. At times the conveyor belts and passenger searches around her stopped as ad-hoc translators were gathered from their nearby duties. During one of these correspondence deciphering gatherings, she watched in disbelief as a young, uniformed security guard pushed his sleeveless arm through the tangle of officers who were arguing in a mixture of Arabic and broken English. His apparently autonomous fingers flicked open her leather wallet, separated and gripped the paper money within, and disappeared inside the cabal of jabbering airport guards. It seemed to her as though stealing money from visitors here was quite an ordinary thing for Libyan security officials to do. Moments later, the same uniformed official smiled as he leaned forward to examine more of her belongings. She noticed the casual way in which he brushed aside the worn, wooden-handled weapon that he wore over his left shoulder. The assault rifle looked familiar. Hilary Connors' knowledge of automatic weaponry was limited. She couldn't name Sergeant Mikhail Timofeevitch Kalashnikov's world changing invention, but she could recognise the weapon of choice of the child soldiers of the continent she had landed on.

It may have been an inauspicious start to her journey, but, for Hilary Connors, things were going to get much worse. Through the enormous windows beside their incoming visitors' queue the travellers could see the pitiful line of cars waiting to collect them. Hilary was propelled forward in the stampede towards the only manned immigration desk. With an elbow blocking the path of one traveller to her left, and her suitcase fencing in another on her right, she made sure that she was one of the first passengers outside in the ensuing scramble for a taxi.

In the foyer of the Beach Hotel, she was met by a teenager in a white gown with a red stripe down one side. The boy, who was wearing a gleaming white scull cap perched jauntily on top of his tiny head, handed her a bedroom door key. Hilary worked out her room number from the empty space on his key rack and left to find her own way to her room. Unable to locate any functioning lifts on the ground floor, she dragged her suitcase up four flights of stairs and through the thick layer of plaster dust which coated the floor of every corridor. In her half-built bedroom, electricity cables protruded from the wall on either side of the room door. Her bathroom was a small, tiled cubicle with a hole in the floor sporting a brace of footrests. For convenience her private pit had a rusting shower head perched precariously above it. The somewhat disorientated guest organised her belongings as appropriately as she could, considering the circumstances, and ventured downstairs to the restaurant, where a squat passenger she recognised from the flight invited himself to join her. The dark patches under his arms reeked of body odour.

Her short, hairy companion picked his teeth and smiled at her, 'welcome to Libya,' he began, 'the arsehole of the world!'

'Gin and tonic, and lots of ice,' she gasped to the red-striped teenager as he bussed between the tables.

'First time in a Muslim country?' her squat companion asked, twisting his bulky shoulders towards the boy. Seconds later the lad returned with two tall glasses.

'It's a mixture of fruit juices. It's no substitute for a G and T, I'll grant. But you won't find one here, so you'd better get used to it. How long are you staying, anyway?'

'Not sure,' she replied, sipping her drink slowly. 'I suppose it's not bad for fruit juice, but I really do need a decent drink. Can I not get one anywhere?'

'You can always get everything anywhere, if you know the right people. Here,' he added, pushing the menu towards her. 'What are you going to have? Are you a meat eater?'

She nodded.

'Then try the Libyan soup. They serve it everywhere here. It's good. You really ought to try it. My room number is eighty two. Call there at midnight. I'll see what I can do. By the way, what's your room number?'

She hesitated for a moment and then replied, 'forty seven, why?'

'I thought so, I needn't have asked really. The same rooms are always allocated to the unwary.'

He turned once again to the boy, who was busy at a far table. At the sound of his voice, the boy abandoned his customers and ran towards them.

'Follow Farouk,' her companion advised, 'he'll show you to a room on my floor. It's not all doom and gloom in this place; it only appears that way to newcomers.'

He clapped his hands together loudly and the boy led Hilary towards a lift tucked in behind the reception desk.

CHAPTER 9

Farouk stood smiling by the door as Hilary scooped her belongings together. She turned to face him more than once but since he constantly retained the same idiotic, wide-eyed grin, Hilary knew the boy couldn't understand a word she was saying. He took her case, which was almost as tall as he was, and seconds later they had entered a higher, brightly lit, white-walled hallway. If she had not recently escaped from the squalid room below, she would not have been so struck by the soft furnishings which now surrounded her. A gentle, exotically spiced breeze, mildly scented with cardamom, cumin and coriander, touched her face as she stepped out onto her terrace. From the veranda she surveyed the houses below. Each façade was painted blue, brown or yellow. Transfixed, she watched groups of local children shrieking joyfully as they ducked in between the battered, dusty cars, which formed lines on both sides of the street. Above their heads, electrical cables weaved a tangled web from house to house. From somewhere close by came the distinctive, excited, brisk warble of a familiar songbird. As the evening fell, and the daylight faded, the warm twilight air around her filled with the harmonious voice of the muezzin, calling the faithful to prayer.

Then suddenly, her relaxing contemplations were brought to an abrupt end by the harsh tone of the bedside telephone. Moments later, she presented herself, dressed in fatigues before the familiar Texan, in orange running shoes, who propped up the mahogany counter in the foyer.

'Ya'll got over here OK?' he murmured approvingly, leading her into the street. Briskly, and without ceremony, her American guide led her into the heart of the ancient, walled Medina, through a jumble of narrow alleyways. In places all around them the old city lay in ruins. Between the remaining whitewashed houses, passageways curved mysteriously. Many alleys twisted and turned and some simply ended abruptly for no apparent reason. The encroaching gloom which surrounded them was intensified by the shadows cast from the palm matting which hung from arches above their heads. Steering her over a festering rivulet, which carved a path through the mud beneath their feet, the Texan ducked into a dark doorway. Hilary stood for several seconds waiting for him to emerge. Eventually and gingerly she entered the cool, damp passage. To her right a flight of stairs curled into a basement meeting room. Cautiously, Hilary felt her way downwards.

As the door before her opened, she could make out a number of men, sitting silently around a large table in the gloom. As she entered, an unusually tall man at the centre of the table stood and gazed around the room. From his accent it was obvious to Hilary that he was an Englishman.

'All of you here know what I'm talking about,' he said, 'this was supposed to be a short-term scam relying on our experience and our contacts. And it would have worked and it did work, but I told you then and I tell you again, it won't work by simply stealing the money directly from the oil fund. Everyone agreed to put it back after we've regained our investment from each deal. It's working capital, that's all. We always did that and that's why we've never been caught. You all know our basic idea was to get political favours and oil contracts, then sell them on to legitimate oil traders. In the process every single one of us in this room got large kickbacks from the competing oil companies. It made everyone in this room a lot of money and it was so simple! What this really means, and every single man in this room knows it, is that the US government has no problems with us all robbing South America, Nigeria and Middle Eastern countries blind. We can take whatever we want from whoever we want, and we do. Who here doesn't know about the recent US big oil scandals?'

Not a single man in the room volunteered to display his own ignorance.

'Who isn't familiar with the fraudulent Halliburton subsidiary's redevelopment contracts? Who knows nothing about what went on between the Mobil Corporation and Kazakhstan's oil minister?'

Again, no-one drew attention to his lack of knowledge.

'We all know that's why our oil firms usually sign lots of secrecy clauses. And why we're ignoring the British government's transparency initiative.'

A murmur of agreement passed around the room.

'But, we all knew our government would come after us with everything it had if we dared to steal straight from the US tax payer and we agreed not to. But since we began operating this year, four billion dollars have vanished out of the fund. A government

34

investigation into that missing money is due to start in two weeks time.' He paused. 'And you know where it's going to lead to, don't you?' The speaker paused again and then turned to face Hilary's guide. His audience turned with him, so that the whole room was now staring directly at Hilary and her companion.

'To him!' The speaker pointed at the centre of the Texan's chest.

'Listen to me!' he called out, his voice rose sharply as he spoke. 'None of us has done anything illegal. Morally, we're all implicated, but all we did was make money. Isn't that what our country's all about? But listen, I urge you, get out while you still can. If the authorities contact you, co-operate with them as much as you can. Remember, all any of the rest of us has done, is follow the American Dream. There isn't anything wrong with that.'

The baffled conspirators divided into small circles, where they huddled together whispering. The Texan approached the table.

'Ya'll know I didn't take any of that money out of that fund!' He laughed and spread his arms, as though bearing himself to their scrutiny. 'C'mon now, ya'll know me better than that!'

Their eyes followed him around the room, as he squeezed towards his accuser. Attaching himself to the speaker's shoulder, he waited for his colleague to lower an ear. For a few seconds the pair held a private but involved conversation. The Texan turned the other man towards a doorway at the back of the room and they both departed. Somewhere in the far passage one of the men flicked on a bare electric light bulb. Cast in the harsh glare of the naked bulb the two shadows circled each other. Around Hilary, nobody moved or spoke, until one of the far off men fell to his knees. The other raised an object high into the air. From the shadow thrown against the wall the victim could be seen covering his head with his arms.

CHAPTER 10

From his visit to Hilary Connors' doctor, Simon Hawthorne knew that her terrible scar injuries had been sustained during her marriage. The doctor wasn't sure when. He knew that Hilary had been treated privately. The physician expressed no view about Keith Connors' neglect of Hilary's wellbeing. But it had been evident, to Hawthorne, from the man's discomfort, that the idea of shielding Connors, however indirectly, from the all too evident effects of his brutality, was a task that he did not relish in the slightest. The doctor could have made excuses for Keith. He might have mentioned how much strain Hilary's husband was under at that time. But he didn't. And Simon Hawthorne was well aware of the meaning of his host's silences.

Hawthorne added yet another enquiry to the list of things he needed to ask Hilary. He had already begun to form an impression of Keith brutishness. And, if his picture of the man was accurate, then it seemed to him as though a powerful motive was obvious. And it also seemed clear to him that all of his recent enquiries still pointed towards a single woman. And that woman had vanished.

A superintendent entered Simon Hawthorne's office. Detective Superintendent Tony Jarvis was fat. He'd spent a lifetime behind a desk, and it showed.

'Don't get up, Simon,' Jarvis panted. 'I just wanted to find out if everything was going according to plan. No problems with the investigation?'

Hawthorne smiled, 'well, my chief suspect has decamped, sir,' the detective admitted, as if it was news.

The superintendent already knew. Everybody in the police station knew. But nobody had any idea where Hilary Connors was.

'Yes, I gather the victim's wife has disappeared, together with her passport,' the superintendent continued. But he didn't look concerned. 'It's a simple enough matter to deal with,' he muttered. 'We know exactly who we're looking for. Don't we? We'll do the

36

usual nationwide radio and television appeal. Then we'll check passenger manifests for airlines and ferries and trains. We'll find her in no time. You mark my words.'

It was Jarvis' way of trying to cheer him up. But Hawthorne wasn't cheered. People weren't travelling. Even someone as new to murder as Hilary Connors would know that. It was obvious. The streets in every city were deserted. If she turned up at a major port or airport and asked for help leaving the country she'd stick out like a sore thumb. Hilary had gone to ground somewhere. That much was plain to everybody. And it suggested at least a little forward planning on her part. So he didn't share Jarvis' confidence that the woman would be found quickly.

They were joined in the room by Hawthorne's detective sergeant, Dalgliesh. He was a tall man, much slimmer than the man he stood next to. Side by side the pair reminded Hawthorne of Laurel and Hardy. He laughed.

'That's the spirit,' Superintendent Jarvis boomed.

'It's down to brass tacks then,' the black detective declared clearing a space on his desk for his sergeant. 'What have you got for us?'

'I've been to Mrs Connors' bank,' Dalgliesh explained. 'There were several transactions for large amounts of money, but we seem to be able to account for everything which Hilary Connors spent. She took ten thousand pounds out of her account on two separate occasions last month, and then a few days later, she put the money back. Whatever she took out, she either spent or returned. I looked for signs that she paid an assassin, but there were none.'

In his mind Hawthorne was running through all the things he needed to check. He needed to speak to her friends. He'd spoken to her son. The list was endless and time was running out. There was one thing, however, which stood out from all the rest. He'd found a phone number on the victim's body.

'It belongs to someone we've arrested for indecency and obscene publications offences,' the detective explained to Sergeant Dalgliesh.

'Are you're saying when he died Keith Connors had the phone number of a pornographer on him?' the sergeant asked.

'Not only that,' Hawthorne continued. 'Do you know who this is?' From his desk drawer he pulled a set of high-quality photographs. The naked woman the images depicted was well-known in their town.

'Of course I know who that is!' Dalgliesh exclaimed. 'It's Nancy Collimore. Do the images and the phone number go together?'

The inspector could almost see Dalgliesh's mind working. An obvious line of reasoning presented itself. Mick Collimore, the naked woman's husband, had a fearsome reputation. He'd been convicted of several murders and remained locked inside a maximum security prison. The photographs might potentially lead them to a motive for murder. But the obvious suspect couldn't have committed the crime, because he was in gaol at the time.

'Do you think Collimore ordered the killing from inside, sir?' Dalgliesh asked.

'I don't know,' Hawthorne admitted. 'But whether he did or not, we've got to talk to the man who produced these photographs.'

The semicircle of Potter's Yard craft shops, which lined the cobbled market terrace, had their brightly varnished Dutch doors open at the top and closed beneath. Hawthorne entered the print shop in the centre and was met at its gleaming, pale, wooden counter by a middle-aged man in jeans. The shop owner's smile faded as a large group of uniformed officers crowded into his small doorway.

'You might want to close the shop for a while.' Hawthorne advised him, producing a search warrant from his breast pocket.

The owner nodded and did as he was told.

'It's a nice place you've got here,' the inspector declared. 'I remember when you used to develop your dodgy porn photos in a cupboard under the stairs. I see business is good these days and life has been treating you well. I want to ask you some questions about Keith Connors.'

'Oh God!' the shop owner replied. 'What's he done now?'

'He is dead,' the detective said. 'He was murdered yesterday.' The shopkeeper looked first at Hawthorne and then at each of the uniformed officers in turn.

'Oh no,' he said. 'Not me!'

'Did you take photographs of Mick Collimore's wife?' the detective asked before the pornographer could regain his composure.

'Of course I did,' the photographer admitted.

'Did you know at the time when you photographed Nancy Collimore naked that her husband was dangerous?'

'Of course I knew. Everybody knew that Mick Collimore killed his enemies.'

'How did Collimore find out about the pictures?' the detective probed. The shopkeeper repeated part of the policeman's question to himself out loud as though he was having difficulty understanding it.

'Oh no,' he said at last. 'You've got it all wrong. If you think I had something to do with Keith's death there's something you should know. My business was financed by Keith. Without his help I couldn't run this place. There's something else you should know too. Years ago Hilary and Nancy posed naked for me all the time. Nancy's husband always knew what kind of a woman she was. Selling their work was my main source of income. Hilary stopped working abruptly. She married Keith and he invested in my business. He said financing me was conditional on my staying out of contact with his wife. I would have done that anyway, but I wasn't about to turn down his money.'

'Where to now, sir?' Sergeant Dalgliesh asked as the detectives left the photographer's shop.

'It looks like Keith Connors was murdered by a professional killer,' the inspector explained. 'We need to find out why. Who paid for the murder to be carried out? If Keith wasn't the only target then we need to find out who the others are and warn them of the danger they're in.'

CHAPTER 11

Luke Connors was not apprehensive about the prospect of hearing his father's will being read out. He and his father had never been close. In fact, there had been a degree of animosity between them. And, subsequently, he felt nothing in particular. The air was cold, so he hurried. The bright, red-brick offices in the centre of Andall's Commercial Dock Way business park seemed inviting to the young student. And the prospect of a hot drink encouraged him.

He approached the downstairs reception desk in the office of his father's solicitor. There a young receptionist smiled as he approached.

'I've come to see Mr Cardman,' he said, hesitantly.

Accordingly, the girl telephoned ahead. Two floors up, a dark-suited, balding man, in his late fifties, met him at the lift door.

He extended his hand, 'Mr Connors, may I call you Luke? First of all, let me say how sorry I am about your father, we all are. I understand how devastated you must be.'

Luke made no reply. Instead he smiled. The lawyer sat Luke in a leather Chesterfield chair facing a large, antique desk. Behind it, filling a mahogany bookcase sat row upon row of dark, hide-bound legal volumes. Cardman brought an empty chair and placed it close by.

'We have much to cover and we won't get it all done today,' he said glancing at his watch. 'Nevertheless, there's nothing stopping us covering the rough outlines. We can go over the details later, as you wish. Are you ready?' He paused, 'good. The first thing I should say is that, as your late father requested that I execute the terms of his will, I'll now read you the terms of that will: *'To my son, Luke Connors, I leave my house, its grounds and its contents and the business in its entirety.'* Your father had already made provisions for the administration costs. There is one other matter which I must alert you to. Your father and I worked closely with an accountant, his name is Delatouche. He has something important to tell you. May I invite him in?' Anticipating his new client's approval, Cardman lifted the receiver before him.

'My mother?' Luke murmured. 'What about my mother? Didn't Dad leave her anything at all?'

'I'm afraid not,' Brian Cardman acknowledged. 'No, I'm afraid he didn't.'

Luke frowned.

'Well, why not?' he snapped. 'Why the bloody hell not?'

The solicitor didn't have a chance to answer Luke's previous question. At that moment the office door opened, and Keith Connors' accountant entered the room.

Delatouche looked about the same age as Luke's host. He was thinner though, but similarly attired. He rubbed both palms along the outsides of his jacket before shaking hands with Luke and sitting down.

Following the customary condolences, he began, 'Mr Connors, may I call you Luke? Has Brian told you anything about Colombia?'

The student shook his head.

'I'm sure you were aware that your father and his American associate spent last winter developing a project in Colombia. Anyway, the hard facts are that the research they were carrying out was not entirely permitted, neither by the British government nor by the American one. It appears as though a substantial sum of money was diverted from your father's company's operating account and paid to this man here.' He showed Luke a name printed in the heading of a company letter. 'He's one of America's leading oil developers and is considered by some to be the father of America's oil lobby in Washington. From what we know about this man, it's most likely that money found its way into an American political campaign fund. I must say, that's not unusual. The long and short of it is that we're as certain as we can be that almost all of the things we have told you about were improper. When I say improper I mean illegal. And we are taking steps to recover your father's money.'

Luke walked slowly to his father's house in Saint Anne's Terrace. Until that moment, he hadn't thought particularly hard about who might have killed Keith and why. Throughout his life he had been conditioned not to concern himself with a subject that his father had always referred to as 'the harsh reality.' It was a curious philosophy. In fact, it was partly to blame for the Connors Family schism. It simply meant that Luke found Keith cold, insensitive and unappealing. When he was alive Keith had always prided himself on his realism. And he'd done his best to instil a hard-headed attitude in his only son which would one day rival his own. Perhaps he'd even succeeded. Luke liked to persuade himself that he was indeed nothing at all like his father. But, in reality, perhaps he was far more like the man he despised that he would ever admit.

All of the police crime-scene marking tapes had been removed. The house was now his. He closed his front door and scribbled himself a note, '*find bicycle, walking sucks*'. From the half of his father's DVD collection which he had spread across the carpet, he pulled the film *Apocalypse Now*. He'd watched the film, the filming details and reached the middle of the director's cut before he began to feel drowsy.

The room about him was almost completely dark. Its only light came from the flickering television screen. He wasn't sure what had woken him up. His first reaction to the sound of scraping across the kitchen work surface was surprise. Almost asleep, he wandered towards the kitchen and reached for the light.

Instinct, more than anything else, prompted him to call out ahead of him, 'is anyone there?' He flicked the light switch but nothing happened. The stairs behind him creaked. Something moved ahead of him. Then hinges of the sitting room door squeaked. Luke grabbed the lamp from the table in the centre of the room.

'Get away from me!' His voice was shrill. The flex from the light came away from the wall as he backed towards his father's fireplace. He couldn't see anybody, but he knew people were there. The outline of a stranger advanced towards him in the flicker of the television's harsh glare.

'Don't come any closer!' he shrieked.

The figure moved forward.

'Ya'll don't wanna go on in getting involved in stuff that don't concern you none,' a voice cautioned from the kitchen.

'Go ahead, Vince, ya'll wanna show him.'

Luke anticipated the blow. He stepped aside. The flex caught as he swung the lamp. The first punch sent him sprawling into the fireplace. He didn't remember any of the other blows.

42

CHAPTER 12

All the time that Luke lay on the floor, he was conscious. He was pretty sure the men who had attacked him had gone. He couldn't hear movement. He tried looking around once, but the agony from so doing gave him the idea that he should keep his head still. As the ravages of pain racked his battered body, Luke sprayed clusters of coherent words into his father's telephone. In short order, after that he heard a knock at the door.

'It's the police,' a voice called out. The visitor directed a beam of light toward his face. A second torch beam appeared some way off and an older voice asked, 'what happened to you, sir? Can you stand?' The older policeman examined the student and announced, 'no bones broken! You've been in the wars, lad. Do you want to tell us what happened?'

'There were three men in my house and they attacked me,' Luke said. As the student spoke the house lights came on.

'I've fixed the fuse,' the young policeman called out.

Luke recognised the uniformed officer who had taken him to the police station some days earlier. He had the same smile this time.

'Three?' the sergeant asked. 'You saw three? Can you describe them?'

'No,' Luke admitted. 'The house was dark. But one man had an American accent and the one who attacked me was called Vince. They said something about my not interfering in their business.'

'We'll call our inspector. He'll investigate your attack, sir,' the officer explained.

'Can you tell me if anything was taken?'

At the top of the stairs Keith's office door stood open. The young officer entered it. Everything in the room was orderly except for a wheeled suitcase which stood beside Keith's desk. It contained maps, charts and engineering drawings most of which had been pulled apart and strewn across the floor.

'I've called the inspector,' the older policeman shouted up to his colleague at the top of the stairs. 'Don't touch anything, Andy.'

43

Inspector Hawthorne entered through the open front door.

'There you are, Luke, what happened to you?'

'This is nothing really, you should've seen the other guy!' Luke replied and tried to laugh. The swelling on his upper lip made it impossible.

The uniformed officers and their inspector conferred. Hawthorne was at once both impressed, and concerned by Luke's forbearance and his bravery. He wasn't sure, at this point, if the youngster realised how precarious his situation was. And regardless of whether Luke was aware or not, Hawthorne didn't want to alarm him further. It seemed obvious to the detective that his charge was having difficulty assessing the situation. His father had been murdered, possibly by, or at the behest of his mother. And now she was a fugitive from British justice. And he, himself, had been beaten up, very possibly by the men who committed the murder. If that wasn't a terrible predicament, Simon Hawthorne could hardly imagine a worse one. But he was mindful to show neither pity nor condescension to the young man.

'Listen carefully, Luke, and tell me if I get anything wrong,' Inspector Hawthorne instructed. 'There were three men in your house. You're sure? All were upstairs when you got home. In the dark they told you not to meddle in things which didn't concern you and then attacked you. What had you been doing?'

'I hadn't been doing anything,' the student insisted. 'I went to see Dad's solicitor and then I came home. That's it.'

'Who is that?'

'Brian Cardman.'

'Your father conducted risk assessment surveys, for oil companies, didn't he?' the detective asked. 'Did you ever meet any of the people he did business with?'

'None,' the youngster admitted. 'But Dad's solicitor did tell me this afternoon that father had some financial arrangement with an American. He said it was to finance a political campaign, or something. To be honest, he was a bit vague. But he told me whatever had gone on, they'd recover Dad's money and pass it back to me. So I had nothing to worry about.'

'Did Mr Cardman actually use those words?' Hawthorne asked with a look of surprise. 'I mean, considering the circumstances, he might simply have wanted to sound reassuring.'

Luke Connors watched Hawthorne's face changing. 'No-one has been reassuring me,' he explained. 'I'm simply being logical.'

The detective rubbed his forehead. 'Logic might help,' Hawthorne reasoned. 'But, don't you find it difficult to reason effectively whilst considering your parents' predicaments?'

Everyone in the room could see that Luke was thinking. The two constables who had found Luke on the floor were staring at him. Their sergeant ushered them out of the house. It seemed obvious to Hawthorne that Luke was aware that convention required him to express grief, bereavement and confusion. But Luke Connors appeared to be far from conventional, because he showed none of those things.

Simon Hawthorne frowned. He knew that his face was contorted, and he tried hard to relax. He wanted both to comfort Luke and to extract information from him. In common with every detective, Hawthorne knew about the difficulties of such an endeavour. And, like the others, he also knew that the most awkward and invasive questions often produced the most useful results.

'Forgive me,' he said. 'I take it that you and your father weren't all that close.'

'Not especially,' Luke replied, without flinching.

Hawthorne waited. He was expecting Luke to deny any knowledge of the circumstances surrounding his father's death. Luke wasn't obtuse. And Hawthorne assumed that it must have been clear to him what his indifference was implying. The denial never came.

'Who profited from your father's death?' Hawthorne prompted.

'I did, exclusively,' Luke replied. 'As of this morning I'm extremely rich.'

Again Hawthorne waited. Finally he spoke. 'You don't have anything against the police, do you?' he said. 'You don't bear any grudges against us. You wouldn't want to trick or mislead us in any way would you?'

It was Luke's turn to look surprised. 'I don't know what you mean,' he exclaimed. 'Who's misleading whom, and about what?'

'That's the saddest thing of all,' Hawthorne agreed. 'I really do believe that you actually don't know what I mean.'

'Well, what do you mean?' Luke demanded.

Hawthorne smiled. 'We can't both ask the questions,' he explained. 'That's not how this process works. Did your attackers carry anything with them when they left the house?'

'I don't think so. Why?' Luke Connors replied.

'Because they seem to have been interested in your father's engineering drawings. We can't tell if they took anything because we don't know what was there to begin with. Do you mind if I take what's left back to the station? One more question before I go. Did you tell anybody that you were going to see your father's solicitor?'

'No,' Luke replied. 'Why?'

'Nothing really,' Hawthorne admitted. 'It's just a bit puzzling, that's all. These people knew what they were looking for. And having so recently been a crime scene, this house might seem a risky one to break into. It's got uniformed officers only a few meters outside the door. And yet they did just that twice, once in order to attack your father, and then again in order to attack you. Where did he work mostly, your father?'

'He worked all over the world,' Luke explained. 'Wherever you find oil basins you'd find my dad. I suppose that's true of all people like him. Like many consultants of his type he worked for several famous oil companies. But he stopped for a while once.'

'Oh?' the detective exclaimed. 'When was that?'

'I was about ten at the time. It was the year that the Shell Oil Company pulled out of Nigeria. Being a risk assessor it was Dad's job to advise the company. There was a huge public outcry because someone famous had been executed to protect Nigerian oil interests. His name was Saro-Wiwa. My father said at the time the things people said about the oil companies' ruthless methods were all lies. If they were lies, the lies caught the imagination of people all over the world. Ken Saro-Wiwa's death caused a great international scandal. Most people have forgotten about it now. I remember my dad telling me that what the oil companies did was justified, but at the same time he couldn't find any work. I think the oil companies blamed him personally for all the adverse publicity.'

CHAPTER 13

At first, in the Libyan cellar where Hilary had attended her oil industry meeting, nobody reacted to the violent act being carried out in front of them. The whole group of technical specialists simply sat and stared. Then suddenly, everything happened at once. Because she was nearest to the door and already half-facing the stairs, Hilary Connors was the first person to reach the street. She ran, at first not always in the same direction, and then, later, she simply ran away. In the old part of Tripoli, where she was, gullies ran down the centre of each passage. She made no effort to avoid them. All too soon, Hilary was splattered with foul smelling substances that she couldn't identify. Turnings led nowhere. Roads were blocked by houses. Hilary retreated again and again. She was totally lost, bewildered and dishevelled. And it wasn't until she was completely out of breath that she thought suddenly of finding an ambulance for the victim. Hilary couldn't speak Arabic. It was unlikely that they, whoever and wherever they might be found, would speak English, and she was covered from head to foot in something awful. The more she considered summoning help, the more unwise the idea seemed. And, although this time, and in this city, Hilary hadn't actually done anything wrong, she felt more frightened and exposed than she ever had done in her home town.

She took a deep breath. The air was fetid. Standing with her back straight, she brushed herself down a little and began to walk purposefully. She felt reassured. While setting off, Hilary noticed splatters of her blood upon the backs of her hands. More drops fell from her forehead. A head wound, which until that moment had seemed painless, now began to throb. Her breathing was beginning to return to normal when she first spotted a figure advancing towards her across the closest expanse of derelict waste ground. There was no escape behind her, in that direction lay the cul-de-sac from which she'd come. To reach the nearest alley on either side would necessitate approaching the figure. She slipped behind the remnants of a crumbled wall and hid.

'What on earth are you doing down there?' the advancing stranger asked.

'I was hoping to hide from you,' she replied, 'I might not have been so elusive had I known you were English. Who are you anyway?'

'Major Carter,' the stranger replied, holding out a hand. 'You look as if you could do with a guide.'

'How did you know I was here?'

'Simple, I followed you. I was in the cellar. When I saw you I was naturally curious. We don't often get beautiful women joining our secretive, subterranean gatherings. If we hadn't been so packed in, I'd have introduced myself earlier.'

'How did you know where I was going?'

'I saw you run straight into the gutter outside the vault and then flee towards both of the dead ends in the adjacent streets. The others and I know this area. I didn't think you'd get far and indeed, here you are. By the way, we take care where we step here in the old town. Bodily waste runs in the centre of these streets.'

She let the stranger pull her to her feet. 'Oh, God, I'm sorry,' she gasped withdrawing her hand quickly. 'You wouldn't happen to have a tissue or know where I could wash a little, would you?'

For a moment, they simply stood together in the lamplight thrown from a nearby window.

'I think I know just the place were there's water,' he began and then added, 'it's ironic, isn't it?'

'What is?' she asked, surveying her mottled figure.

'Water in the desert. Here we are, cutting each others' throats in the hope of prospecting for oil and this country's greatest engineering feat has nothing to do with us or oil. It's its water system!'

'I haven't cut anybody's throat,' Hilary insisted. And then she reflected that indirectly she had. But she recovered quickly by adding, 'what were you saying about the water?'

'It's fantastic!' the major explained. 'It's one of Libya's greatest triumphs. They've sunken a pipeline into the dessert, to transport hundreds of millions of gallons of water. The Man Made River they call it. It's the eighth wonder of the world, the largest engineering project ever completed.

'I could find a use for a million gallons of water,' Hilary quipped, drawing attention to her clothing with a sweep of her right hand, 'I mean, look at me!' She paused, 'I'm sorry, this is not your fault.' She reached out to touch his arm, thought better of it and straightened the front of her blouse instead. 'I'd better clean myself up. Which way then? After you. Are you an engineer yourself?' Hilary asked, feeling awkward after her outburst.

'Yes and no,' Carter replied. 'I qualified as a civil engineer before joining the army.'

Major Carter led her across Tripoli harbour onto a narrow, wooden walkway. Ahead of them, the splendidly illuminated Maltese ferry shone out of the darkness. Behind it, in turn, its glow lit up an assortment of half-built fishing trawlers on the far side of the dock. From there, she could scoop sea-water onto her badly splattered clothing.

'You must think I'm awful, worrying about how I look, when there's some poor man lying in God knows what state in a cellar back there, and we haven't done a thing to help him. Do you know what became of him?'

'As I set off after you they were bringing him out onto the street. The first thing I saw was a gash splitting his face from lip to cheek. He was gasping and his face was covered in blood. The others could see that he was gagging and they tried to put him on his side. I've seen similar injuries before when I was on active service, and I knew he was already showing signs of brain haemorrhaging. If an ambulance does arrive, he'll be taken to Tripoli airport, to be transported by air for treatment in Tunisia. But I don't think he'll make it. Most people in his condition never do. We should discuss something else, you know. It doesn't matter what. Look at you, you're shaking like a leaf. You're suffering from shock and exhaustion. Let me get you to your hotel. Where are you staying?'

Squeezed next to Major Carter in the service lift of her hotel Hilary realised for the first time how tiny the space actually was.

'How long did you say you've been here?' Carter asked, surveying the hallway outside their lift.

'I arrived about four hours ago,' she called after him as she struggled with her shoes.

'You've done well. They usually give the worst rooms to new visitors.'

In spite of the major's presence Hilary tipped on her shower and climbed into it, taking her shoes and clothes with her.

'I'll leave you in peace then,' the major called from her doorway.

'No, wait!' she shouted, catching the shower curtain and pulling it around herself in a peculiar manner. 'I mean, can you wait?'

'I'm right here. Is there anything you need?'

She didn't reply. First she covered herself in soap and scrubbed. Then she stripped and scrubbed. He knocked on the door.

'Is everything alright in there?'

'It's fine. It's all fine,' she replied, waving a hole in the vapour cloud. 'Don't come in, everything's just fine.'

CHAPTER 14

'We've got engineering drawings from the victim's house and some of them are old, sir,' Sergeant Dalgliesh told his inspector.

'How old?' Hawthorne replied.

'Some were drawn in the Eighties,' the sergeant explained. 'He's got plans of drilling sites as far afield as Alaska, Nigeria and Libya, sir. Whatever it is we're looking for, we're going to have to narrow our search down.'

'We've got to start somewhere,' Hawthorne agreed. 'Let's start with Alaska, for no other reason than that the plans from there are the most recent ones.'

'And the wife?' Dalgliesh commented. 'Where does she fit in?'

'It's hard to tell,' Inspector Hawthorne admitted. 'We believe the killing was done professionally and Hilary had no large sums of money missing from her bank account. We also know from Luke that he, not his mother, benefited from his father's death. From what we know about her she's unlikely to have known how to contact an assassin on her own. And we know that she knows nothing about oil exploration.'

During their discussion Superintendent Jarvis joined the detectives.

'Don't mind me. Carry on,' he insisted.

'I looked into the Ken Saro-Wiwa killing in Nigeria, sir,' Dalgliesh ventured. 'It was Greenpeace who accused Shell Oil of indirect culpability in his execution. But at his trial Saro-Wiwa pointed the finger at the company directly. He said the damage they had done to his people and the Niger Delta would be judged by the whole world after his death.'

'What do you think we're looking at in this victim, Keith Connors?' the superintendent mused. 'An oil developer with a conscience? And, what about the son? You told me he was a bit of a cold fish. Couldn't he have done it?'

'Not the shooting, no, sir,' Hawthorne explained. 'During the murder Luke Connors was asleep in Manchester. I've spoken to the family who gave him board and lodging. And, judging by the parlous state of his student finances I'd be very surprised if he could have interested a professional assassin at any time in the recent past.'

'So where does he fit in then?' Jarvis grunted.

'That's what I'm trying to work out,' Hawthorne sighed. 'Being emotionally deficient is hardly a crime, is it? If it was, we'd have to lock up a fair proportion of the nation, I'd imagine.'

'You're saying that the son didn't like his father, but he didn't kill him, then?' Superintendent Jarvis summarised. 'Well, somebody did, didn't they? We know that Hilary Connors was no professional assassin, don't we? And somebody obviously did the job for her, didn't they? Who could have put a normal, Andall housewife up to a stunt such as hiring a professional assassin? Let's face it, it's not the kind of topic that you'll find being discussed by the checkout in Budgen's Supermarket, is it? Can't you find out who his oil ventures upset? Can't exploring that avenue help to explain how old scores get settled in the oil industry?'

'Well, we know he worked everywhere,' Hawthorne explained. 'We know for instance that last year he was in Colombia advising their state-owned oil company, Ecopetrol, when one of their leading oil trades unionists, Rafael Cabarcas, was shot.'

'What are you saying?' Superintendent Jarvis blurted out. 'Are you saying that Keith Connors, an oil industry risk analyst, was actually advising these oil companies to kill their political opponents?'

'No, sir, I'm not,' Hawthorne explained. 'I'm just pointing out that he was there during these events. That's all. We don't know what advice he gave his clients. That's something we're going to have to find out. But if he did tell them to assassinate local activists and they did so, they're hardly likely to admit it.'

'What then? Are you suggesting that this might have been a revenge killing?' the superintendent persisted.

'Yes, sir, it probably was. Nothing that I've heard about the man recommends him to me. He crushed his wife almost to death. And when we found his body it had the telephone number of a known pornographer on it.'

Superintendent Jarvis snorted.

'Oh, I see! Lazy police work, is it? Blame the victim, and all that?'

'No, sir,' Hawthorne countered. 'I'm not blaming the victim for anything, at least not yet. All I'm saying is that I don't like him very much! But, in any case, irrespective of how much I may or may not like what I've heard about Keith Connors, so far, I still can't imagine why someone bent on revenge would break into the victim's house and steal his drawings. And why warn Luke not to meddle in things which didn't concern him? If any of these things are connected, and I'm not suggesting that they are, it might suggest that Keith was killed to keep something quiet. My question is what?'

'Isn't it unprofessional of you to approve or disapprove of the dead man, Inspector?' Jarvis snapped.

'Yes, sir, it probably is,' Hawthorne conceded. 'But I can't find it anywhere in my soul, regardless of how professional a soul that is, to admire a man who beats and wounds his wife, and lives off immoral earnings!'

Superintendent Jarvis shuffled around before changing the subject.

'That reminds me,' he volunteered. 'Have either of you heard of a man called Paul Frank Whittler?'

'I haven't,' Hawthorne admitted. 'Why do you ask, sir?'

'He's gone and got himself killed, apparently, somewhere in Libya. Anyway, I got a call from the Foreign Office about ten minutes ago asking whether or not his name had come up in regard to your investigation.'

Hawthorne frowned.

'Nobody knows about our investigation, sir,' he protested. 'It's hardly started!'

The superintendent pointed to a flickering television across the hallway in the staff canteen.

'The news report's coming up now,' he explained.

The three officers crossed the hall to stare at the screen. In the centre of the picture before them a journalist stood in a street in Tripoli surrounded by flashing lights.

'There has been no official comment from Washington on this story yet,' he said. 'But we understand from sources here in Libya that the US Trade Representative has been murdered. We did contact the White House Press Office, but they wouldn't speak to us. If the victim does turn out to be Ambassador Whittler it'll be an enormous blow to the United States. Whittler has been instrumental in repairing the damage done to the relationship between the two countries in the Nineteen Eighties, by the Berlin nightclub bombings, the subsequent US raid on Tripoli and Lockerbie. Since September The Eleventh Libya has shown common cause with the US and a grateful senate has called for ties between the two nations to be strengthened. Paul Frank Whittler's death will undoubtedly be a huge setback both to this administration and to the president himself. The two men are known to have been close friends for many years.'

'Did the Foreign Office say why they thought this man's name might have come up in our inquiry, sir?' Hawthorne asked.

'Yes, they did, as a matter of fact. The clerk I spoke to simply said that Whittler had appointments with Keith Connors and that it was our duty to establish whether or not these appointments had been kept.'

The detectives laughed.

'Did he really say it like that?' Dalgliesh asked.

'Yup,' said Jarvis, smiling. 'But he did seem concerned. I promised to look into it for him.'

CHAPTER 15

'Do you want me to question Mrs Nancy Collimore about these pornographic photographs, sir?' Dalgliesh asked his inspector. 'We know Keith's job took him all over the world. We can tell that from his drawings. We know he worked in some dangerous places like Bolivia and Colombia, but my instinct tells me that his killer came from much closer to home. An obvious explanation is simply that Mrs Collimore's husband found out about her and Keith's pornography business and had him killed. The man's a convicted murderer after all.'

'We'd be neglecting our duty if we didn't at least interview the woman,' Hawthorne admitted, reaching for his coat. 'Come on then, Sergeant. Let's get this over with.'

The two men walked up the short asphalt drive outside Mick Collimore's house. Nancy Collimore answered the door in a cream-coloured, lycra bodice which emphasized her lithe figure. She paused with the door open as she scanned Dalgliesh's face.

'You, I know,' she murmured in Hawthorne's direction. 'But this one's new to me and he's a handsome devil, isn't he?' Then she leaned across the doorway. 'Is this about Mick?'

'No, actually it's you we've come to see. This is a bit delicate, I'm afraid. Can we come in?'

Nancy led them into the kitchen as her daughter entered the room from the main part of the house. The girl had the same dark eyes as her mother and a similar mischievous grin which seemed to be permanent.

'Go on, there are no secrets between me and Moni, are there love?'

Hawthorne coughed, 'perhaps another time would be more convenient?'

Nancy took the hint and changed her mind, saying, 'Moni, love, why don't you and Charlie take the dogs for a walk?'

Then she waited by the open kitchen door until her offspring were out of sight before continuing.

'She's seen most things, you know. Not much goes on that Moni doesn't know about.'

Nancy then wiggled across the floor between the two men. Her outfit hadn't left much to their imaginations when she was standing still. Now the movements she was making bordered on the seductive.

'Mrs Collimore.'

'Call me Nancy,' she urged, smiling as she approached the sergeant. 'Would you like me to take your jacket off?'

The inspector swivelled to face their host as she minced around the room.

'In our recent investigations we've uncovered certain, how should I put this, revealing photographs of you, which we thought had been taken by Keith Connors.'

Nancy stopped and turned to stare at the detective.

'Revealing photos?' she said. And then her face lit up. 'Oh, you mean my porno photos? Why didn't you say so? You could have said that in front of Moni. She knows all about that.'

Hawthorne rubbed his eyes and continued.

'To put it bluntly,' he said. 'We want to know if the photographs had anything to do with Keith Connors' untimely demise.'

For a moment Nancy Collimore did nothing and then she started laughing, gripping her imitation mahogany kitchen work-surface for support as she did so. 'I need a drink, this is priceless!' she said, crossing over to her fridge, but this time without any exaggerated hip movements. She tipped herself a vermouth and plopped ice into the tall glass from an orange, plastic mould shaped like a fish. Then Mick Collimore's wife pushed a nearby door open with a sandaled right foot. She entered her spacious living-room with the two detectives in her wake. Both sat opposite as she relaxed into a white, leather settee which curved from one corner of the room to the other.

'Keith Connors has come a cropper, and not before time if you ask me. He was a bastard,' she said. 'Are you asking if some old noddy photos of me, you've pulled out from God knows where, had something to do with it?' She shook her head and her eyes narrowed. 'Photos can shock people, especially mine, but they've never harmed anybody. What exactly is it you're really after?'

Hawthorne took another set of photographs from his jacket pocket. These ones showed a teenage girl with two naked, older men.

'What can you tell me about these photos then?' he asked.

Nancy Collimore froze and the colour drained from her face. She remained silent for some time and then stepping over the sergeant's

56

legs to peer around her net curtains she said, 'alright. My kids will be back soon, then you'll have to leave.' She took another large swig from her glass and refilled it, this time without ice. If she'd ever looked sexy in her skimpy bodysuit, she didn't now. She looked frail and frightened.

'I've known Keith Connors for more than twenty years,' she said in a shaky voice. 'I knew him long before he married that bitch. I was on the game. That's how he found me. I did photos for him. You know about that. Not long after that I met Mick at a private party. I had my eyes wide open. I knew what kind of a man Mick was when I married him. He knew about some of my past, not all of it. It suited me to leave it like that. Anyway, Keith needed some money. We both knew the score. So I gave him what he wanted. Mick found out that the money was missing, but he didn't know who'd taken it. I knew what would happen to me when he found out. I'd be killed. I wasn't in any doubt about that, wife or not. You don't steal money from Mick Collimore. No-one does. The only way I could get the money back was to get Keith to help me sell photographs of my daughter. I asked her to pose with different men and she agreed. I was desperate. I had no choice. I didn't know what else to do.'

CHAPTER 16

'So, what's happened to 'don't speak ill of the dead', all of a sudden, sir?' Dalgliesh exclaimed, as the two detectives exited from Mick Collimore's house. 'Everybody is queuing up to explain to us what a bastard Keith was. Even his own son is thrilled to see the back of him. That's not the way things normally work, sir, is it?'

'It's unusual,' Hawthorne admitted. 'People ordinarily at least make an effort to appear civilised, even if they're not. But, I get the distinct impression that Keith Connors was as talented at gathering enemies as he was at gathering fortunes. But, devil or dove, Sergeant, our job is to catch the man who killed him, and the man, or woman, who paid for the assassination.'

'What if they all did?' Dalgliesh asked.

Hawthorne was going to say, don't be daft. He'd managed to get half of the phrase out of his mouth when it dawned on him that the idea wasn't nearly as ridiculous as it sounded.

'What do you mean?' he asked instead.

'We've only been investigating Keith and his family for a day or so,' Dalgliesh explained. 'And already we don't like what we've found out about our victim's personality. They, Keith's family and acquaintances, were all far more familiar with him than we are. They've all had a lifetime of knowing him, sir: Ken Saro-Wiwa, Hilary's scar, the photos. That's what we've discovered, so far, after just one day! What about all of the things that we don't yet know about?'

Simon Hawthorne stopped abruptly. He felt light-headed. But he knew the cause. His loss of equilibrium wasn't brought about by exertion; it was a direct result of fear. If Dalgliesh was stumbling towards a conclusion that Keith Connors had deserved his fate, then it wasn't far removed from a deduction that he, himself, had already made. For a man with his responsibilities such thoughts were unacceptable. And Hawthorne was already painfully aware of his lack of impartiality.

'You can't let such things cloud your judgement!' Hawthorne snapped. 'For God's sake, man, just listen to yourself!'

Simon Hawthorne had never spoken to Sergeant Dalgliesh that way before. In fact, he'd never spoken to any serving officer in such a manner. The sergeant's mouth was open. Dalgliesh simply stared. He was trying to speak. But the words just wouldn't form.

'I'm sorry,' Hawthorne said, quickly. 'I didn't mean what I said.'

'You did mean it, though, didn't you, sir?'

Hawthorne nodded.

And Sergeant Dalgliesh continued.

'You're thinking the same thing.'

Simon Hawthorne would never have admitted that he thought a murder victim deserved his fate. Even if he did think it, he knew that thinking it and saying it were not the same. He glanced at his sergeant. He couldn't tell if Dalgliesh's stare contained defiance, contempt or hurt. It occurred to him that the look he saw might easily contain all three. He considered repeating his apology. He was regretful; it had been as much for his own benefit that he'd warned of the dangers of admitting personal bias into a police investigation as it had been for Dalgliesh's. He'd spoken unjustly. He knew that.

'What I said was wrong,' he said. 'Will you accept my apology?'

Sergeant Dalgliesh averted his gaze.

'It's still there, though, isn't it,' the sergeant observed. 'Apologising to me doesn't make Keith Connors a nicer person, does it? What are we going to do about the fact that neither of us likes him?'

Hawthorne looked at his watch.

'We'd better be getting back,' he said. 'Let's first check on Luke and see if he's heard from his mother yet. The things which Nancy told us could put a different light on Hilary's disappearance.'

Luke answered his father's front door. He looked relaxed.

'Oh, it's you,' he said. 'Come in. Do you know Monique Collimore?'

'We've never actually spoken,' Hawthorne admitted. 'But we know who she is. Monique, how do you do?'

Monique was attractive. She had her mother's auburn hair and dark eyes. Luke filled a kettle and opened a cupboard, while his girlfriend lined a neat row of cups along the kitchen counter.

'Was everything alright with Mum then?' she asked chirpily.

'Everything was fine,' the inspector assured her. 'Tell me, did your mother and Luke's mother get on well?'

'I don't know,' Monique replied. 'I suppose so. I mean, Mum didn't say anything when I told her I was seeing Luke. I think she even told Dad about it, so she must have done.'

'I need to ask you, Luke,' Hawthorne continued, 'has anyone ever threatened your dad that you know of?'

'Of course they have!' Keith's son explained. 'I'm not an expert on South American oil exploration politics, but I know that getting death threats isn't particularly unusual for people who do my dad's job. Last time Dad was in Colombia one of Shell Oil Company's executives got murdered. The man's son explained how their family received a warning by telephone from London the day before it happened. When I asked my dad about it he just said his oil company deals with things like that and that was all he'd say about it.'

'I'll get the details from the police in Bogotá,' Hawthorne commented. 'But specifically, your father, did he receive any threats?'

'Oh yes. They all did, not just my father. It was my dad's job to advise the companies when it was time to get out of a country. There was always a lot of money at stake. On the one hand he had to consider the company's losses, its contractual obligations to local governments and its shareholders' interests. And on the other hand he had to consider how strong local opposition was getting. And that can't be underestimated. You can see that from Ken Saro-Wiwa's comments at his trial. He thought the oil companies were destroying the ancestral homelands of the Ogoni people. Exactly the same thing is true of the indigenous Indians in the Peruvian and Ecuadorian forests. Look what happened there. The oil companies turned tail and fled. Dad was always at the sharp end. People like him always stand halfway between the defeated oil companies and their opponents. There are always threats in the oil business, Inspector, plenty of them, and they're nothing new.'

When the two detectives left Keith's house both of them looked sombre.

'What is it?' Hawthorne asked. 'What's the matter?'

'Exactly how hard are we detectives prepared to work in order to uncover the murderer of a fellow police officer?' Dalgliesh said.

Hawthorne frowned.

'You know the answer,' he complained. 'No killer of a police officer can ever relax. You know as well as I do that the murders of PC Blakelock, and of WPC Fletcher are still the subjects of intense investigations more than two decades after the events. Why are you even asking me that?'

Dalgliesh smiled.

60

'And, if a known drug-dealer, with numerous convictions for an assortment of violent offences, bleeds to death in an alley, how likely is it that his killer will be caught?'

Hawthorne shrugged his shoulders.

'It depends on the evidence,' he replied. 'If there's little or no evidence left at the crime scene, and no witnesses, the killer probably won't ever be caught. What's your point?'

'That's precisely my point, sir,' Dalgliesh explained. 'We sometimes deliberately allow ourselves to fail. That's the simple truth. For our fallen comrades, PC Blakelock and WPC Fletcher, we'll, literally, travel to the end of the world. But for some victims, who are only ordinary members of the public, we won't even interview willing witnesses, even if they come to the police station of their own accord and ask to speak to the duty sergeant; remember Steven Lawrence?'

Hawthorne was angry. He didn't know why Sergeant Dalgliesh was so exorcised about this particular victim. He'd decided that if his sergeant wanted to embark on moral crusades he'd have to find somewhere else to do it.

'Look, Sergeant,' Hawthorne snapped. 'I don't know why you're so concerned about Keith Connors in particular. But we're following the leads. We're interviewing his connections. Whatever the excess personal, and psychological baggage is that you're carrying, I'd be truly grateful if you'd drop it! For goodness sake, we're supposed to act like professional investigators rather than half-baked and simpering agony aunts!'

'It's being true to yourself, isn't it?' Dalgliesh replied. 'It's admitting to yourself when you've declined to make one additional telephone call, or ask for one extra forensic examination. In a word, sir, it's integrity.'

Hawthorne halted. He watched Dalgliesh forging ahead of him. The sergeant didn't look back. Hawthorne didn't know what he'd said in order to bring about such a reaction. He'd instructed Dalgliesh to drop his emotional baggage. He'd shouted about cloudy judgements. But what had he said which had cast aspersions on Dalgliesh's integrity? He felt certain he'd not said anything which had done that. But the sergeant, it seemed, felt differently. Hawthorne now trudged in Dalgliesh's wake. And, as he did so, he reran all of their recent conversations through his mind.

Superintendent Jarvis was edgy when his detectives arrived back at the station having spoken to Luke.

'Do we know whether or not Keith Connors met with the US Trade Representative yet?' he asked.

Hawthorne and Dalgliesh looked at each other.

'We think Connors might have been threatened before he died, sir,' Hawthorne tried to explain. 'Shouldn't we deal with one thing at a time?'

'I need to get the Foreign Office off my back,' the superintendent complained. 'Let's look at this threat thing later. Did Connors speak to this American politician or didn't he?'

Neither of the plain-clothed officers knew the answer.

'The White House Trade Representative has an entire department at his disposal,' the inspector reasoned. 'It could have been any one of them who arranged to meet Keith Connors. In fact, I think one staff member deals with energy and natural resources. Let me look up his name and I'll find out what's going on. I won't be a minute.'

A little later Hawthorne telephoned a clerk from the North American Team of the Foreign Office, in Whitehall, and explained who he was.

'I need to speak to you urgently,' the Foreign Office clerk replied. 'The appointment I'm so concerned about was in Whittler's private diary. You must tell me. Did the two men meet?'

'We don't know,' Hawthorne admitted. 'Do you have any idea what the meeting was about?'

'In respect to Connors, I'm certain,' the clerk explained. 'The appointment was arranged at the height of yet another Libyan scandal. In this fresh round of allegations the Libyan leader himself was accused of backing a plot to kill the crown prince of Saudi Arabia. It's no secret the leaders hated each other. They even traded insults openly in public. Keith Connors had already entered into negotiations with Libya's state-owned oil industry, The National Oil Company. He also advised British companies, who sell to the US, to invest in oilfields which had been abandoned decades earlier. The investments were enormous. With his reputation at stake it's a fairly safe assumption that Keith wanted to know how the fresh terrorist accusations would affect American initiatives to rekindle links with Quadaffi's regime. The short answer is very badly, indeed, despite Quadaffi's strenuous denials that such a plot ever existed. If the fragile international relations couldn't be mended, and it looked increasingly unlikely that that they could be, then Keith and his investors stood to lose billions of pounds and he would be finished.'

'Connors needed Whittler's advice badly then,' Hawthorne agreed. 'It's clear he had a lot at stake. So it's probable that at least he turned up for the meeting. But what about his contact?'

'It would take a brave politician or a fool to be seen doing business with Keith Connors. Are you aware that there have been huge oil scandals in Nigeria and Colombia in recent years?' the clerk asked.

'Yes,' said Hawthorne.

'Did you know that oil companies have been accused of killing trades union activists? Whether or not they've actually carried out the killings is another matter. They've been accused of it. A pattern has emerged. After the first international firms arrived at Colombia's big state-owned oil refineries, the activists who were already there began to be murdered. Scores died. Are you familiar with the facts?'

'Yes,' the detective said.

'Did you know that the risk analyst and strategist for the foreign oil companies in situ, at both of the largest refineries, was Keith Connors?'

'Yes,' Hawthorne admitted. 'We know.'

'That's my problem,' the Foreign Office clerk explained. 'It's understandable that Connors wanted to see Whittler. That much is clear. But Whittler's no fool. What we cannot understand is why such an important US official would agree to meet someone like Connors. Why would anyone in a position like his take such a risk, especially if the advantage to be gained fell only to Connors? And why did they meet privately? We need to find out what Whittler wanted in return and we need to find out urgently. Connors' clients all resorted to violence and intimidation. There's no dispute about that. We don't know if they actually murdered the trades unionists. They all blame the killings on the Colombian army. But the problem with their explanations is that they don't account for the murders that took place in areas where there were no soldiers. The only things we know certainly are that wherever there was a combination of Connors and a new foreign oil company, union workers died.'

Hawthorne was aware of the fact that he was scowling. It was rapidly becoming impossible for him to regard Keith Connors death with any degree of objectivity at all. He knew it. Jarvis knew it, and so too did Dalgliesh. A Foreign Office official had just said that only a fool would openly do business with the man. Nancy Collimore had expressed satisfaction at his death. Doctor Adams had had nothing good to say about him. And, at the very most, his son, Luke, had only expressed surprise at his sire's untimely demise, and not much surprise at that. It seemed as though Luke was not overly keen to disagree with the oil industry's assessment of his father either. During the Saro-Wiwa scandal it seemed perfectly obvious that Keith had been blacklisted. And Luke knew all about that episode. He'd explained it lucidly. But he didn't seem to have the slighted interest in protecting his father's reputation. Hawthorne thought, a little more. Perhaps, he decided, Luke realised that there wasn't much of a reputation left for him to protect.

CHAPTER 17

Hilary dozed among her scattered sheets. Her eyes opened, as somewhere beneath her window an agitated shepherd cautioned his noisy flock. Gradually, as her senses returned, she recognised the Muslim early morning call. Covered by a blanket, the major, set in his chair by the window, looked almost as though he belonged there. A twinge of guilt spurred her on tiptoe towards the shower.

'How long have you been awake?' she asked brushing his arm gently.

'I wondered when you'd join us. I'm famished and I know just the place.'

She flopped onto the sand outside the white walls of the old city, while the major spread out their breakfast between them on the ground. Though still early, the sun already shone fiercely in a cloudless sky.

'Have you explored the market?'

She shook her head and squinted in his direction.

'We've still got time. I need to go to the trade fair. Doesn't your husband have a stand there, too?'

'Oh, God, the trade fair! I was meant to be there!' she exclaimed, returning suddenly to the present. 'What's the time? Which direction is it in?' She wiped sand from her bottom as she stood.

'Don't worry, the taxi will drop us off further down along the waterfront, we can walk from there. Speaking of the waterfront, have you seen the castle?'

She looked directly into his face and turned her mouth up slightly at each corner.

'I thought not. Here, look, just close your eyes and relax.' He straightened her arms. 'From Green Square, we stroll west in this glorious sunshine, under the palms towards Sharaih Omar Al-Mukhtar.' He smiled as she dropped her shoulders. 'That's better. You see there's no rush here. The street is named after the indomitable Libyan freedom fighter, still celebrated as *The Lion Of The*

Desert. His is an inspirational tale of Bedouin heroism and adventure. They made it into a film. I'll dig it out for you, if you like.'

'I'd like that, she replied, smiling. Can I open my eyes now?'

'The Tripoli International Trade Fair buildings are further down here,' he called out from ahead of her.

As they entered the airy and spacious foyer, Hilary began to take in the logos of the British firms, with their advantageous positions next to the entrance. She noticed British Gas and the Anglo-Dutch oil giant Royal-Dutch Shell.

'This way please,' a guide called out channelling the newcomers into the back of an extremely crowded hall on the right. In front of a display marked *Britain's Trade Minister Lord Uxbridge*, a man neither of them recognised was finishing his speech.

'...We have at last begun a new start in co-operation between our two countries. The break in ties between our peoples and our governments had lasted longer than was necessary.'

'It's upstairs,' she whispered, tilting herself forward to reach the major's ear.

There were far fewer people on the floor above, nevertheless an impressive number had still gathered. The major scanned the room as Hilary pushed her way forward.

'This is Christopher Delatouche, he used to be Keith's accountant, Major.' She looked behind her, where her companion had been until a few seconds earlier. The man behind the Connors Enterprises stand had his back to her and was bending down. Suddenly, a firm hand gripped her elbow.

'There you are, Carter, what were you doing over there?'

'We have to leave, now!' the major insisted.

'What on earth are you talking about? We've only just arrived. Look, I was just going to introduce you to my husband's accountant.'

The major pulled her towards one of the emergency exits.

'Ouch, what's the matter? That hurts!'

'I don't know exactly, there's something not right. I can't put my finger on it. I've felt it many times before and it's always kept me alive. We've got to leave and we've got to do it quickly.'

'But what about the company? What about the exhibition? I can't just leave. I've come all this way. Nothing's going to happen here, for goodness sake! It's a public place. Just look at all these people!'

People around the couple froze as she pulled her arm away from him. Then, straightening her jacket firmly with both hands, she took a deep breath and strode towards the stand.

'Hello Christopher, I'm glad you're here. I was afraid I wouldn't see you,' she called out to the figure inside the stall. A man she had never seen before turned and straightened. About him, the contents of the stand were strewn.

'Hey, wait a minute!' she exclaimed running towards him. 'You're not Christopher!' He stared at her, and then exchanged a signal with someone standing inside the main entrance. Walking directly towards her, the stranger nudged his jacket, revealing a pistol handle, protruding from a leather holster. At the same time he raised a finger to his lips. He passed inches from where she stood and then, together with his companion at the door, he descended the stairs calmly, and strode outside into the street.

'We're attracting unwanted attention, we have to move to one side, now,' the major urged, gently steering Hilary towards the emergency exit.

A tall, olive-skinned man in a pin-striped suit, who had been standing beside Hilary seconds earlier, gathered a group of bystanders around him and pointed in their direction. Her heart-rate slowed steadily, as they merged with the other visitors on the stairs.

'Let's return to Green Park and sit down. We'll decide what to do from there in a moment,' the major cautioned, as he walked on the outside of the street sheltering Hilary beside the tall buildings. 'Who do you think would be interested in rifling through the belongings of Connors Enterprises? It's not a well-known company.'

She stopped and stared at her companion. 'How did you know something was about to happen back there?'

'I didn't know what was going to happen exactly, but I was looking for the security guards or policemen in the building. It's a part of my job, it's also something of a habit. They're normally standing by entrances or exits. If they're not there, they're often either completely absent or patrolling. At first I noticed a dark-clothed figure that I took to be a security guard standing by the entrance. He looked away from me as I studied him, which is unusual, security guards are used to being noticed, they're often prominently positioned or formally dressed and they don't tend to react much when you study them. This one did. At first, I wasn't unduly perturbed, I just thought he was odd. And then I noticed him signalling to a man on the far side of the room, the opposite side from your business stand. It was after that, when both men looked directly at me, that I knew something wasn't right. I just didn't know what it was. I thought...' he stopped.

'You thought what,' she coaxed, gently.

'It's nothing, really.'

'I won't understand unless you tell me,' she insisted.

'Alright, at first, I thought they might have been looking for me. Of course no sooner had I considered that possibility than I dismissed it. I didn't know I was going to be here today, so they couldn't possibly have known. The only other alternative was that they must have been looking for you.'

'What are we going to do now?'

'First you have to tell me what you're running from. If you don't, I can't help you.'

'What, now? Here? I can't just blurt everything out. You never know who might be listening and in any case I hardly know you.'

'I don't want to pry into your affairs any more than I have to, believe me. And in any case, I ought to abandon you really, but I'd never forgive myself if I did. You obviously need my help. You might think you're doing a good job of hiding whatever it is that's troubling you, but believe me, you're not. Let me share a couple of my observations with you. On the night I met you, you ran from the scene of a gruesome murder, I can't fault you for that. But you didn't make any attempt to contact the embassy or report the crime in any way. Nor did you make any mention of my failure to report it. And now you've been threatened by a gun in a public place, but once again you make no attempt to report it. I know there are people who say they 'don't want to get involved'. That usually means they fear reprisals, should it ever become known they gave information to the police. If I'd guessed you were such a person, I'd have expected you to leave the country. But you're still here. I suspect that you might somehow be in trouble and you need to avoid the authorities. At first, I was puzzled by the fact that you seem to be cautious in this country, despite never having been here before. Then it occurred to me that whatever your secret is, it might have been shared among many separate police forces by now. You can't return home, either because you need something here, or you fear being caught if you do, perhaps both. How am I doing so far?'

'I'm tired, I need to lie down,' she replied.

'Do you know which way you're going?'

'I think it's this way,' she replied, waving her right arm weakly and sitting on the back of a public bench.

'What are you waiting for?'

'Aren't you coming? I can't tell you yet. I'd prefer it if you stayed with me though, are you coming? You don't have to sit in the armchair all night. I'll swap with you if you like.'

He covered her left hand with his right, 'I'm not going with you, Hilary, I'm sorry, not unless you tell me what this is all about. I know you need help, you had *help me* written all over you from the first moment I saw you. But it's much more than that, isn't it? And I need to know what I'm getting myself mixed up in. You can try lying to me if you like. But you'd better do it quickly, because whoever it is that's looking for you will find us in this square soon enough.'

She sniffed, pushing her index fingers against her temples and with her open palms covering each cheek, she created a set of blinkers. From below her wrists, he watched her tears chase each other to the base of her chin and drop into the dust at her feet.

'Can't you just see me back to the hotel and stay with me until I find Christopher?' she pleaded. 'I'm in trouble, you're right about that, but it's not something you need to be afraid of. You've been with me this long, just a couple more days, that's all I need.'

'I'm sorry,' he replied, 'I don't mean to be harsh but there's something about me you don't understand. I'm also at risk here, well, not just here, everywhere. You could say I work for a security firm. The point is I need to be able to assess what the risks are all the time and that's something I can't do with you, if you won't tell me what I need to know.'

'But I don't know you. How do I know you're who you say you are? If I tell you, how do I know you won't hand me in or try to harm me in some way?'

'You don't. Look, you've got a choice. Either you work out a plan on your own and make an attempt to carry it out or you take my offer of help. The question is, are you going to survive on your own? You've got to take a gamble, the decision is something I can't help you with, save but to say, you have to make your mind up right now.'

CHAPTER 18

There was one person in Andall who knew how Keith Connors' business affairs worked. The last person he'd tell anything to was Hawthorne. The detective knew that. But he was hoping that Keith Connors' solicitor would unintentionally reveal clues about his secrets when responding to questions. If Hawthorne could spot unease or difficulty in answering, it would help his investigation a little. He really needed anything and reading body language was better than not doing anything at all.

'How can I help you, Inspector?' the solicitor began as Hawthorne eased himself into a low, leather Chesterfield chair.

'How much can you tell me about Keith Connors' business affairs? Before you answer, I'm not asking you to breach client confidentiality. If it helps, Luke Connors has already told me about some missing money which might have been given to an American election campaign.'

At first, the solicitor made no reply. He aimed his narrow, brown eyes down at the inspector. With his chin tilted upwards towards the edge of the mahogany desk, the posture of his host reminded the detective of a hawk judging the distance towards its prey. 'What exactly has my client been telling you?' he mused.

Simon Hawthorne took his notepad from his breast pocket and flicked over a succession of pages. '*My father had been in Colombia during the winter of 2002, according to Mr Cardman. He and an accountant called Delatouche discovered that there were some irregularities in Dad's accounts.*' He stopped reading and added, 'I think that's what he said.' And then from the text, he continued to read, '*a considerable sum of my money had been inadvertently donated to the campaign of the Republican Presidential Nominee James Landale. My accountant is trying to recover it.*'

'Do you mind if I take a quick look at your notes?' the solicitor asked, holding his opened left hand towards the detective.

'Perhaps later,' Hawthorne replied with a smile, as he returned the notepad to his pocket.

'Yes, of course, how clumsy, Inspector. You really must excuse me.' He looked at his watch, 'We don't have much time. What exactly is it that you wish to know?'

'Did Keith Connors ever mention feeling threatened or being followed? And did he ever entrust anything to you for safe-keeping?'

'I don't believe he did, Inspector. He was quite a well-balanced man, not one given to starts or flights of fancy.'

'It wouldn't have been fanciful for a man to feel threatened had he anticipated his own violent death, Mr Cardman, surely?'

'Perhaps,' his host replied abruptly, surveying his watch for a second time and rising towards his office door. 'Now, if there's nothing else I can help you with,' he said. 'I'm awfully sorry to hurry you, but I really must get on.'

The detective retrieved his notebook for a second time and studied its pages for several seconds. 'You know, there is one last thing that you could tell me before I leave. Do you know the petrol workers' union in Colombia?'

'Not personally, no. Why? Should I?' Brian Cardman asked with a look of surprise.

'I suppose you'll be unacquainted with the fact that one of its leaders was murdered during a protest against the Colombian government's industrial reforms?' the detective asked.

'I would, yes,' Cardman admitted. 'I don't know anything about Colombia or its oil industry.'

'Then you'd be surprised to know that the man responsible for the killing telephoned Keith Connors here in your office a day earlier, I expect,' Hawthorne said triumphantly. And there it was. For an instant Brian Cardman lost his composure. Hawthorne studied his host's worried face as he desperately tried to remember which phone call was being referred to.

'I think I've taken up too much of your valuable time already, Mr Cardman,' the inspector said before his host had had time to recover. 'Thank you so much for agreeing to see me at such short notice. I'll see myself out.'

Dialling his sergeant's number as he pushed open the foyer door, Hawthorne trotted down a set of imitation marble steps onto the street. Instinctively, the detective surveyed the outside of the building. He knew Cardman was watching him as he hurried away.

There was an unusual tremor of excitement all over Andall Road Police Station as Hawthorne climbed the stairs to his office.

71

'Ah, there you are, Simon, I've been looking for you,' Superintendent Jarvis called out to him. 'The briefing is in twenty minutes. Where have you been?'

'I've been to see Luke Connors' solicitor, sir,' Hawthorne replied, as the superintendent began descending the spiralled stair case.

'Any news on the two women yet?'

'Not yet, sir, no. I've applied for a warrant to search the Collimore house. I'll be appearing before a magistrate in two hours time.'

'Well done, Inspector,' the chief replied, altering his course and returning to the top of the stairs. 'Still, it's a pity we didn't take this course of action sooner. But then, you know what they say, better late than never. Twenty minutes, Inspector.'

Dalgliesh and Hawthorne met at the entrance to the inspector's office. By now Hawthorne was in quite an agitated state.

'I think I've got them!' he told his sergeant. 'I don't mean just Connors, I think I've got Brian Cardman, too. I'm almost sure that when he wanted his legal position verified, Keith Connors set up office at Cardman's place. He seems to have been taking and receiving telephone phone calls there routinely.

I think when the time comes, and we study Mr Cardman's bank account we'll find that Keith Connors was not an ordinary client and Cardman didn't charge him by the hour as you or I would expect. And I think I know something else about them, too. I'm not exactly sure of all the details, but I think they accepted money on behalf of several oil companies and sent it straight into the republican presidential campaign fund. The donations were far too big to have been made by an individual. It's simply a trick. Lots of firms stopped giving money directly to political parties after the Enron scandal. But individuals, as always, are free to do what they like.'

Sergeant Dalgliesh said nothing. He didn't enter Hawthorne's office. He hovered in its doorway.

'Did you want something?' Hawthorne asked.

'It's all changed,' Sergeant Dalgliesh replied. 'A minute ago Keith Connors was a ner-do-well, who got what he deserved. And now, hardly a second later, he's at the centre of an international investigation. I just don't understand it, sir. That's all.'

'I thought you'd be pleased,' Hawthorne snapped. 'I thought that's what you wanted. You'd better come in, and shut the door, Sergeant. I really don't think that I understand you.'

Dalgliesh had his arms folded. He pushed Hawthorne's door to with his shoulders.

'There's nothing to understand.' Dalgliesh protested. 'All I want to know is who killed Keith Connors, and why. That's what I get paid for, and that's all I'm trying to do.'

'Don't you give me any of that pious crap,' Hawthorne snarled.

Superintendent Jarvis glanced towards the men. And Hawthorne paused to let their superior officer walk further along the corridor, out of earshot.

'You lectured me on the subject of integrity. What the hell was that all about, then?'

'Me?' Dalgliesh spluttered. 'You were the one who talked about cloudy judgement making!'

'And what about making that last phone call,' Hawthorne insisted. 'What about arranging the extra forensic tests which you were so concerned about? Did you really mean any of that? Or was it all just so much hypocritical hot air? I've made my visits and phone calls, Sergeant. What have you been doing?'

CHAPTER 19

Hilary had to make her mind up quickly. She couldn't survive in Libya on her own. She didn't speak the language. But admitting what she'd done to a near stranger was too much to ask of herself. She only had a few seconds. She removed her hand from her face, wiping her cheeks as she did so. On the far side of the square, beneath the archway leading to the market place, a car passed slowly. At first, it paused and then gradually as it followed the smooth curve in the road, it turned in their direction. Her companion looked towards the oncoming vehicle.

'I've got to go now,' he said gently, 'good luck.'

'It's about my husband. I killed him, or at least I think I did,' she volunteered, following him rapidly.

When she didn't continue he added softly, 'I'm sorry, you're not making much sense, surely you either killed him or you didn't?'

'I arranged it, well, what I mean is, I sort of arranged it.' She was almost running in order to keep pace with him. The major stepped into the road without looking, his attention was focussed behind them.

'I met a man who agreed to kill my husband. He said he wanted twenty thousand pounds and he'd tell me where to leave the money. I withdrew the amount he said he wanted and waited, but the instructions never came. Two days later the police told me that my husband had been killed. I couldn't let them arrest me. But if I go back, now that I've neglected the payments, I'll be killed by the same man who killed my husband, he left me in no doubt about that.'

In a recess beneath the high sandstone walls separating the square from the souk, he asked, 'how did you meet this killer then?'

'It was all arranged for me. Christopher told me who to meet, where and when. I just had to make sure I got there on time, and explain when Keith would be in.'

'Keith, Keith who?' the major stopped to ask.

'My husband's name is Connors. As you know, I use my maiden name,' she explained.

The major's demeanour had changed completely now. He had turned to face her. 'Did you plan this?' he asked.

'Christopher told me to leave all the arrangements to him. He'd take care of everything.'

'I'm with you so far,' her companion agreed, 'but that doesn't explain why you wanted your husband dead in the first place?'

Stepping further into the hollow between the walls and the street, Hilary pulled the major closer. She opened her blouse, revealing part of the scarring on her ribcage and lower back.

'I'm not going to tell you everything, not now anyway. I've told you what you wanted to know. Maybe I'll tell you the rest sometime, maybe I won't. Can we go now?'

'If I'm going to help, you have to tell me everything,' the major insisted. 'The hotel's this way. Come on.'

Hilary followed the major into her bedroom. She sat on the bed as he wandered around the room.

'Tell me,' the major said. 'Did Keith or Christopher ever mention a doctrine of any sort to you?'

Hilary put her shoes on the floor and looked up. 'Doctrine? What doctrine? No, I don't think so.' She paused as people passed outside her door. 'Are we safe then?' she asked, covering her face with a pillow. When he didn't reply she sat up and reached for her bathroom cup.

'That illegal alcohol is almost neat. Go easy on it, for God's sake,' he cautioned, stepping out onto the balcony. 'Come here, please.'

She joined him on the terrace, offering him the cup, which he refused.

'This Christopher character,' he began, closing the glass door, 'tell me about him.'

'What do you want to know about him?'

'Tell me everything, we've got time.'

'Christopher Delatouche is a fifty-year-old accountant. In his time, he's been a stockbroker and a finance director. Do you want me to go on?'

He smiled.

'He worked for my husband on and off for years. Until a couple of years ago I hadn't met him. My husband won a big contract and had a celebration. I didn't want to go, as it happens. We argued and I went and the funny thing is, I met Christopher.' She sipped from her glass and he watched her carefully.

'And then?'

'Well, for a while nothing. He came to the house about a month later to collect some paperwork. We couldn't find it. It was another of Keith's late nights and Christopher said he was hungry, so I cooked dinner. I hadn't cooked anything for so long, I needed to look in a recipe book. I put a dress on. I didn't want anything to happen, if you know what I mean, but I was enjoying myself. I hadn't enjoyed myself that much for years. Am I making myself sound like a simpleton?'

'Of course not, but I think I can guess the end of this story. So tell me, once you and he finished your evening together, what did you do after that?'

'We started meeting at a flat owned by one of his friends. The flat didn't have a phone and for some reason I never understood Christopher bought himself a pre-paid phone and insisted on calling me with it. He told me his wife checked their itemised phone bill and he didn't want our conversations to show up on it. He always told me when we were going to meet each other and I was always there.'

The major nodded, 'when was this, exactly?'

'About a year and a half ago.'

'You kept on seeing each other all that time?'

'Well, not just that, we started talking about marriage. He wanted to start again and so did I. I bought my own house and I wanted him to move into it, but he said he couldn't.'

'What about the house? What did you buy it with?'

'My own money, I've always had an income from my family. Money was never a problem for me. It was always a problem for Keith, he was always terrible with money, that's what he needed Christopher for.

Christopher and Brian, Keith's solicitor, went to school together. They've always been best friends. Keith was blackmailing Brian, but Christopher would never tell me why. He hated Keith as much as I did, in fact, I think he hated him more than I did. Keith was an absolute bastard. Christopher didn't want me to confront Keith about the blackmail, he said it would make things worse. He always said the best thing I could do was watch and wait. I wanted to divorce and re-marry as soon as possible, but Christopher kept saying we should wait. He had the whole thing sorted out. And then one evening, just as the trouble began with the fuel crisis in England, he told me to meet a friend of his in the car park at the centre of town.

He told me that we were going to get rid of my husband and that I should follow the instructions he gave me. You know the rest.'

'How often did you see Christopher after this plan was hatched?'

'I only saw him once after that. He said it was better if we only met in Libya, until it was all over and he took my phone back.'

'I suppose you've got no letters and no record of any phone calls. Have you got a photograph of you and Christopher together or presents of any kind?'

She shook her head.

'Did he ever give you anything?'

'He was always very careful about things like that. He said we should celebrate everything in one glorious event, when it was all over.'

'I'll bet he did!' the major commented acidly, taking a swig from Hilary's glass.

'What's that supposed to mean?' she retorted, following him inside the room.

'Nothing, I'm sorry, forget it.'

'Tell me,' she continued.

'It doesn't mean anything, I'm sorry I said it, just forget it.'

'Tell me!' she shouted, banging the glass on her dressing table.

'I can't be certain about any of this, so I'd rather not say anything.'

Hilary snorted and wiped her face with the back of her wrist. Then she raised the glass.

'Alright, look,' he consented, catching her wrist and leading her back onto the veranda. 'I think you've been conned. I'm willing to bet, for instance, that the flat you met in was rented and that there never was an accommodating accomplice. You haven't got any evidence that this affair ever took place, because Christopher wants it that way. You think you arranged to kill your husband but I'm willing to bet that the whole thing had already been set up long before you were consulted. The police will believe you killed your husband, partly because you believe it yourself. Your biggest gift to them so far is that you've run off like a real guilt-ridden person ought to. They'll catch you eventually. You'll confess and after a while you'll tell them about Christopher. But there'll be no evidence that anything you say about Christopher is true and he'll deny it. He'll deny the relationship ever happened and he'll say your story about him having arranged a contract killer for you is simply a fantasy. By the way, this flat, it wouldn't happen to have a drive-in garage would it? And Christopher wouldn't have tinted windows in his car would he?'

'Yes, why, what difference does that make?' she asked.

'It simply confirms my suspicion that he wanted to come and go without being seen, so that nobody would be able to witness the fact that they saw you together.'

Hilary raised the glass above her head, 'you absolute bastard!'

The major made no attempt to defend himself as her blows rained down on him.

'He loves me! You bastard! He loves me! Get out! Get out!' she pushed him towards the door.

He walked around the sea-front three times before climbing the stairs to her room. At first there was no answer at her door.

'Go away,' she replied at last.

He sat outside beside the fountain. Sometime later Hilary touched his head.

'I'm sorry,' she said softly. 'Are you coming back up?'

CHAPTER 20

The next morning, they returned to the major's favourite cafe, sheltered beneath the ancient walls of the old city.

'What do you want to do now?' she asked him as he poured bitter coffee into her tiny mug.

'It's up to you really, what did you plan to do if things went wrong?'

'We didn't actually plan anything. Christopher told me to come here and meet him at the exhibition stand, so that's exactly what I did.'

'I don't want to sound too alarmist, but I'm pretty confident that he never intended to meet you. It could also help to explain why there were men waiting for you. There are one or two things I don't understand though. The first is who were those men at the exhibition and why didn't they take action against us? Mind you, it was probably too risky. Had you been alone, maybe they would have. And then, why were they ransacking your stand? It seems like an odd thing to do in a public place.' He rubbed his forehead vigorously with the open palm of his right hand. 'It's all odd, when you think about it.'

She watched him anxiously as he broke from rubbing his head, to push the end of his pen through the sand.

'This is hopeless,' Major Carter exclaimed suddenly, 'we've got far more questions than answers. I think all the agonising we're doing is actually making our predicament worse rather than better. To improve our situation, we need to think of one simple objective and achieve it. First we must clarify for certain whether this Christopher of yours is your enemy or your friend.'

'I believe in him, Major. We both know he got involved in something dangerous at home. But I know which side he's on. You've got me talking about sides and enemies already.'

'It helps to keep things as uncomplicated as possible. The word enemy is an extremely useful one for simplifying things. Is there anything else, besides your engagement with Christopher, keeping you here in Libya?'

'Nothing, I suppose I can just leave. He instructed me to follow the Texan and meet him here. The Texan has disappeared, presumably fearing trial and imprisonment for murder and we can't find Christopher.'

'But you can't just leave, can you, at least you can't simply return home?'

'Why not?' she asked, raising her head to study his face.

'Because of the obvious danger that you are already in. Christopher or his Texan accomplice may want you silenced. You are a witness to murder, after all. Unfortunately, I suspect that's not the only crime you know too much about. You know of dates and places where the men met, which cars they drove and many other things. These things might not seem significant to you, but I imagine that the police would be extremely grateful for any details they can get. He'll be conscious of the things you know. He's also acutely aware of how vulnerable you are, especially out here where you know no-one and are unfamiliar with the language and customs. Ultimately, I don't know whether your naïveté will turn out to be a good thing for you, or a bad one, all I know is, it would place you in considerable danger the minute you turned up where they'll expect you to be. Do you have anywhere you can go which no-one else knows about, especially not Christopher or any of his friends? Before you answer, I don't want to know where it is, rather, I particularly do not want to know where it is.'

She thought for some time. 'Yes, I suppose I do.'

'Well, in that case, get your things together and go there now.' He crossed the road to the café and returned with a small piece of paper. 'Here's the number of my satellite phone, call it in by-weekly intervals for an update. What's Christopher's home address?'

She shook her head, 'I think he and his wife were moving when we met. We only ever saw each other at the flat.'

'What about his car registration number?'

She shook her head. 'I never took much notice of it.'

'OK, give me as many details as you can. Write down anything you can remember, about conversations, family, likes, dislikes, anything and the address of the flat where you used to meet. I'll start looking there.'

She put her hand on his, 'why are you doing all this for me? I've got nothing to give you.'

'Believe it or not, it's quite simple. You're in distress and I'm helping you and this happens to be my line of work, well roughly, anyway. And in any case, I found you intriguing from the moment I saw you, I can't imagine not helping you.' He drained his cup, 'there you are now. You let me worry about my motives. You've got enough to worry about, getting yourself out of this sorry mess in one piece. Let's just assume for a moment that everything I've said turns out to be right. Things for you become much simpler: There will be two main obstacles, firstly, is there a contract killer waiting to bump you off the moment you set foot in Andall? The other, less serious problem is the police investigation. Find a good solicitor and do everything he advises you to do. That should take care of that. If you've told me everything and you've not missed or forgotten anything important, you'll probably be fine. I'm not a solicitor so I can't really comment on that sort of stuff. The contract killer aspect of things is more tricky. If he exists and has already been paid, unless we get to him before he gets to you, you can't ever go home. If you ignore that very real prospect, you'll have made a fatal mistake.'

They stood together and she kissed him.

'It doesn't feel right at all, my leaving this all to you. Isn't there something I should be doing?'

'Like what?' he replied, 'you can't really interview the two men involved because they got you mixed up in this in the first place. You could fly straight to England and take your chances. But then again, you can do that later anyway, if things don't improve. If you tuck yourself out of the way for long enough for me to make some enquiries and I find nothing, since no-one knows where you are, including me, you can consider the risks on your own and fly to England whenever you like.'

'I suppose you're right,' she replied softly. 'It still doesn't seem right, somehow, but it does make sense.'

'Well, so long then. I hope we meet again in happier times. Don't lose that number, whatever you do. I'd copy it down elsewhere, if I were you.'

'Well, goodbye then, Major Carter, thank you for everything.'

The major smiled as she began to walk towards the hotel.

It didn't take Hilary more than a few minutes to pack her belongings together. She gave the room one last once-over and pulled her case to the lift. Farouk appeared promptly when she rang the bell. The wide-eyed boy nodded enthusiastically when she asked him for the bill. Eventually, he responded to her writing mime. He led her to a comfortable chair and motioned for her to sit down. After a few minutes Hilary retrieved a novel from her case. She was surprised by the sight of a highly polished pair of black shoes which appeared under the bottom of her book.

A stern voice asked in perfect English, 'Miss Hilary Countevèche?'

'Yes', she replied.

'Would you come with me please?' The policeman picked up her case and carried it to the waiting van. He opened the rear door and stepped aside to allow Hilary to climb inside and then he followed her and closed the door. Slowly and quite gently, the battered, grey van pulled away from the front of the hotel.

CHAPTER 21

'Come in, Simon, I didn't expect to see you again so soon. What can I do for you?' Nancy Collimore said propping herself against the inside of her door frame. Her bare tanned legs parted slightly as she measured the inspector's face. Then, leaving the door open so that he could follow her, Nancy twisted through her kitchen, at once, both opening and closing her silk kimono. She knew the detective could see her naked torso in the reflection in the innermost kitchen door. He looked embarrassed.

She settled herself on a tall, darkened birch stool on the inside side of her mahogany-effect kitchen counter and waited for him to settle down.

'You didn't tell me what you were after, Inspector,' she reminded him. And then ran the sharp, lacquered point of her left index finger slowly down the inside of her raised, right wrist. Her robe was still slightly open and she fiddled with it. At that moment two uniformed constables appeared in her doorway. Nancy stared at them and then snapped her kimono shut.

'I thought for a second you'd come to see me,' she said. 'You haven't, have you?'

'I don't know how best to put this,' Hawthorne began, before she could regain her composure. 'It's an awkward question, but do you mind if we search your house?'

Nancy twisted her mouth in a disapproving manner. 'Of course I don't mind. You're wasting your time though. You won't find anything incriminating. My husband doesn't live here even when he's out of prison. Which he almost never is. He's never even been in this house.'

'I haven't come about Mick. It's you I've come to see,' Hawthorne told her. 'Where were you all of last Wednesday evening?'

'I was here,' Nancy said. 'I've got two children to look after. Remember? Why?' She reached for her transparent kettle and pulled a rainbow-coloured, china mug closer.

'Wasn't that the night Keith was killed?' she said. 'But I thought...' she stopped. 'I didn't murder Keith! You don't even think I did, do you? Hey, wait a minute! What is it that you want?'

'It's just routine,' Hawthorne explained disarmingly. 'You won't even know we've been here.'

Nancy sighed, opened a cupboard door above her head and pulled out a tall glass. The detective glanced at his watch as his hostess filled her beaker with Cinzano. It was half past eight in the morning and far too early for vermouth. He rubbed his eyes and said nothing.

'Why do I always need a drink whenever you come near me?' Nancy complained. 'The only other person who does that to me is Mick and I haven't seen him for years!' 'Can you keep a secret?' she asked, pursing her lips.

'Well, that depends on what it is,' the inspector replied, frowning. 'What is it?'

'Come and look. It's kosher. I know. I checked.' At the doorway to Nancy's pink bedroom a camera greeted them.

'You're on film,' she explained. 'Look, let me just type a message to my website customers. Otherwise they won't understand why you're here. They might get the wrong idea about us and ask us to have sex.' She smiled and then added. 'And that would be awful, wouldn't it?'

The detective pretended not to notice. Nancy opened a nearby wardrobe door revealing a computer, more cameras and a large range of latex costumes. Hawthorne rubbed his eyes and said nothing. Nancy's quiet voice returned.

'You won't tell Mick about this, will you?' she said.

'No,' Hawthorne promised. But Nancy wasn't reassured. She was biting her lower lip.

'But what if I have to go to court as a witness or something? He'll find out then, won't he?' she insisted.

'If this is the only dodgy business you've got in this house then he won't find out,' Hawthorne explained. 'You won't have to go to court and Mick doesn't have to know anything.'

Nancy was drinking again. Her mascara had run, making her look like a sad clown. She teetered out of the room and he followed her. In the room next door a uniformed constable was making piles of underwear and sex aids on the bed.

'Right, sir,' he began when Hawthorne appeared. 'I've found...'

'Give me those and get out!' Nancy screamed, snatching her lingerie from the constable's hands. The young man looked at Hawthorne for direction and he smiled.

'Come on,' he said quietly. 'I think we've got everything we need.'

'What was that, sir?' the constable asked as they climbed downstairs. 'Why didn't we do a proper search?'

'We don't have a warrant,' Hawthorne told him. 'We've been invited to search and now we're being invited to leave. So we're leaving.'

For two whole streets as they walked back to their police station the constable said nothing and then he asked, 'sir, if we didn't have a warrant, why didn't we get one? If she knows we're onto her she'll move whatever evidence she's got hidden, surely?'

'She hasn't got any evidence, Constable,' Hawthorne explained. 'Look, it's quicker this way. Her husband is a psychopath who kills people because he enjoys it. He knew the dead man and so did she. We have to investigate her. It's as simple as that. We wouldn't be doing our jobs if we didn't. There we are. We've done it. Now we can concentrate on catching a real villain, and that's all there is to it.'

CHAPTER 22

'How are we going to investigate Whittler without the help of the Americans, sir?' Dalgliesh asked with a look of concern etched across his face.

'I can't answer that,' Hawthorne confessed. 'It's been worrying me, too.' Then he laughed. 'If I knew who they were, I'd ask Whittler's enemies. He was a successful politician, so he must have had more than his fair share of them. If we can track those people down I'm sure they'd be only too delighted to wash Ambassador Whittler's dirty laundry in public. They'd be able to damage their opponents and get a feeling of moral superiority all at the same time. I ask you, Sergeant, how often does an opportunity like that come along?'

Superintendent Jarvis shouted an instruction across the hall to the sergeant. Hawthorne looked up.

'You'd better have a look at this, sir,' Dalgliesh said and crossed into the canteen on the other side of the building. When Hawthorne arrived the two men were watching a news bulletin.

'BBC News Twenty Four has heard from sources on Capitol Hill that Paul Frank Whittler had been indicted for fraud in Nineteen Ninety Five, but that the case was never brought to court. In a leaked report from The Foreign Office we've also learned that officials here had been warned about him on two occasions. The report mentions a British businessman called Keith Connors. In a bizarre twist BBC News has learned that Keith Connors was also murdered two days before the killing of the senior White House official. It's still not clear who's conducting the investigation into the death of Ambassador Whittler, but we know Andall police are investigating the other murder. We'll bring you the details from that investigation as soon as we get them.'

'Don't say anything to any reporter who asks you to comment on this murder case,' Superintendent Jarvis instructed his detectives. 'Leave it to me. Can you bring Mrs Collimore in?'

'Yes, of course,' Hawthorne replied and frowned at the same time. 'What exactly is it that you want me to do with her?'

'You told me that she shared a history with the Connors woman and the dead man, didn't you?'

'She does,' Hawthorne agreed.

'And you said that she called Mrs Connors a bitch, but that she's happy for their children to go out with each other, didn't you?'

'Yes,' the detective admitted.

'There you are!' Jarvis said triumphantly. 'She's hiding something. Bring her in.'

'I don't understand, sir,' Hawthorne protested.

'Just do it!' Jarvis snapped. 'I don't have time to answer questions now. I want her brought in.' Hawthorne fetched two off-duty constables who were getting ready to go home.

'We have to bring someone into the station,' he told them. 'We'll be on foot. I'm fairly certain there will be cameras outside when we get back. No-one is to say anything to the press. Is that clear?' The men nodded.

The street outside their station was completely empty as it had been for days. With Dalgliesh a few steps behind, Hawthorne set off towards Nancy Collimore's house at a fast pace. At the head of his small foot patrol, Simon Hawthorne rapped on the Collimore's patio entrance. Nancy held the door half open and wedged herself in the gap.

'It's you again,' she called out, 'What is it you want this time?'

'I have to ask you to come with us to the station,' the inspector told her.

'What for?' Nancy asked opening her door to let the officers in. 'What is it that you want?'

'We need to ask you some questions,' Hawthorne explained. 'It's just routine.'

'Can't you ask your questions here?' she replied, as she passed a large bag from her freezer to her microwave. 'I'm just in the middle of cooking. I'll tell you anything you want to know. You know that, don't you?'

'It's not as simple as that, I need to take you with me, I've got no choice in the matter. I don't want to do this. I know that sounds odd, but it's true. The quicker we get this over and done with the easier it'll be for everyone including you.'

It was clear from the look on her face that Nancy didn't understand the situation. Out of concern and in order to reassure her Hawthorne tried his best to pretend that he did understand it.

'What about my children?' Nancy protested. 'I can't just leave. Charlie's upstairs in his room but Monique is not here, I think she's with Luke.'

'Don't worry, I'll call him,' the inspector said. 'We'll wait here till they arrive. We'll sort this out. Why don't we have a cup of tea?'

'Is this about the photographs?' she said. 'Oh God! She was sixteen. You're not going to take my children away from me, are you? I told you why I did it. I had no choice! He would have killed me! Don't take my children away, please! Oh no! Oh God!'

'No,' Hawthorne replied. 'It isn't.'

But Nancy wasn't listening. Her eyes were wide and staring. She couldn't comprehend anything that he was saying to her. Then, for almost an hour while the two uniformed constables stood outside, the detectives and Nancy nursed mugs of tea in the kitchen. Nancy drank nothing. Instead she tucked her hands under her arms to stop them shaking.

'Mum, is everything alright?' Monique exclaimed, bursting through the door behind the two policemen.

'I think so, love,' her mother replied unconvincingly. 'I've got to go down to the police station. Can you make sure Charlie gets his tea and stay in the house for me?' Nancy's youngest child entered the room and simply stared at everybody. His mother's pleas for him to go back upstairs went unheeded. He was rooted to the spot.

'What's all this about,' Luke demanded. 'She hasn't done anything. What are you taking her for?'

'I'm sorry. I've got to,' Hawthorne insisted. 'Come on. Let's go,' he said to all the others.

'What are you taking her for?' Luke persisted, stepping sideways to block the entrance. The two constables who were standing outside the house looked in over his shoulders. Hawthorne shook his head and they retreated.

'Please stand aside,' the detective warned. 'You're not helping. The longer this takes the worse it'll be. Get out of the way!'

Luke Connors looked at Dalgliesh whose face was completely expressionless, and then at Monique who had her back to them. She'd started to divide the food her mother had removed from the freezer. She didn't want to turn round in front of her little brother because floods of tears were streaming down her face.

CHAPTER 23

'You'd better come and have a look at this, sir!' Dalgliesh cautioned as Hawthorne passed Nancy Collimore a polystyrene cup. In the police canteen, the two detectives squeezed in behind seated rows of uniformed officers in time to see their superintendent, in his full uniform, take his place on a stage in the centre of a live television broadcast.

'My officers,' he began, 'have made good progress on the Connors murder case. So far this has been a difficult investigation and I'd like to pay tribute to the fine men and women who've worked so hard to get us to where we are now. We believe this was a cold and calculated, premeditated killing and together we are endeavouring to reveal the motives behind this shocking murder. You'll understand if I don't give out any of the operational details on live television. But I can say that we already have a number of suspects in custody at the moment. I'll be able to reveal more at a later date. Thank you.'

'So that's why the superintendent was in such a hurry to get Nancy Collimore in for questioning!' Hawthorne spat in disgust as they left the canteen. 'This has nothing to do with police work. It's pure politics! He must have been planning to make this announcement all the time. All Nancy is doing is feeding his publicity machine.'

Dalgliesh closed Hawthorne's office door.

'I'd keep your voice down, sir,' he said. 'What do we do now?'

Hawthorne didn't reply. He was muttering to himself and shoving pieces of paper around on his desk. The uniformed officers at the other end of the hall had turned their attention away from the television screen and towards the inspector's office.

'If the super wants to direct this investigation towards the Collimores, we'll be forced to spend weeks if not months or years chasing shadows until the whole shambolic investigation gets conveniently forgotten,' Hawthorne grumbled. 'Everybody knows that professional killings are among the hardest of all crimes to solve.

But we should at least be making an effort to solve it, instead of trying to bamboozle the general public by conducting bogus interviews on random suspects.'

Dalgliesh smiled.

'What's the matter?' Hawthorne snapped. 'Have I said something funny?'

'Integrity, sir,' Sergeant Dalgliesh replied. 'Not long ago you asked me whether or not I believed in it. And now here you are complaining that the superintendent's broadcast doesn't have any. Integrity isn't something that you can turn on and off, like a tap, sir. You've either got it, or you haven't.'

'Oh, for God's sake, I'm a full grown man!' Hawthorne bellowed. 'What on earth makes you think that I don't know what integrity is? Of course I do!'

Dalgliesh smiled again.

'Well, in that case, sir,' he concluded, 'the superintendent's political manoeuvres won't trouble you, because you'll be perfectly able to dispense justice single-handedly.'

The men could still see Superintendent Jarvis speaking at his press conference. Hawthorne watched attendant journalists taking photographs.

'But, what's been broadcast is already broadcast,' he mused. 'There's nothing that I, or any man on earth can do to change that.'

'There are people who say that a few innocent people ought to be sacrificed occasionally in order to protect the greater number,' Dalgliesh observed.

'Who says that?' Hawthorne snapped. 'Not you, I suppose.'

Dalgliesh shrugged his shoulders.

'Nancy Collimore has already been sacrificed. Superintendent Jarvis is serving her up to the hungry press-pack as we speak.'

'Not if I have anything to do with it, he isn't!' Hawthorne fumed. 'Come with me!'

'You're not going to say anything to Jarvis, are you, sir?' Dalgliesh cautioned.

Hawthorne glanced upwards.

'Say something?' he mused. 'Say something like what?'

'I don't know,' Sergeant Dalgliesh confessed. 'We've got our work cut out finding Hilary Connors, haven't we? We could just say that. It's not much, sir. But it's still true.'

'To tell you the truth, I hadn't even thought of it.' Hawthorne replied. 'You know Jarvis as well as I do. He knows perfectly well that Nancy didn't kill Keith, we all do! I don't know what he's playing at. But whatever game he's playing you can bet that our opinions about who gets interviewed and who doesn't don't feature very highly in it! And the only way to alter that is to get promoted to chief superintendent! You're not one of those, and neither am I! So until you become one, I'd concentrate on arresting criminals and try your best to ignore the office politics!'

Dalgliesh smiled.

'Right, sir,' he said. 'What do you want me to do?'

'Bring Nancy up here,' Hawthorne replied. 'I'm going to interview her. And ask the duty solicitor to come upstairs at the same time, would you please?'

'This clearly isn't an interview room, Inspector,' the duty solicitor remarked as Dalgliesh set up a tape recorder. Since the neatly dressed solicitor and Nancy occupied Hawthorne's only visitors' chairs, the sergeant remained standing.

'I thought things might be a little more comfortable in my office,' the detective explained.

The solicitor arched her left eyebrow and piled her writing pad and an elongated carton of duty-free cigarettes on the Hawthorne's desk, but she said nothing.

'I've only got two questions; both are about last Wednesday night,' the inspector continued. 'Was your son in the house?'

'I don't want my son brought into this,' Nancy Collimore replied quickly. 'Why are you asking me about him?'

'I've got to do this,' Hawthorne insisted. I won't involve him in anything, or you. Please answer my question. Was Charlie in the house?'

Nancy looked at her solicitor. The woman shrugged her shoulders. 'Charlie was there. He's always there,' Nancy admitted.

Hawthorne smiled.

'That's good,' he continued. 'Now tell me. This website of yours, does it keep a record of what times you and your customers communicate? And did you use it on Wednesday night?'

Again Nancy looked at her advocate. This time she nodded.

'Of course it does,' Nancy explained. 'That's how I know how much to charge people. Yes, I used in on Wednesday. I use it every night.'

'That's all I needed. You can leave whenever you like,' Hawthorne explained, crossing his arms in front of his chest. Both women climbed to their feet. Nancy left the room immediately, but the duty solicitor lingered in Hawthorne's office doorway.

'I don't know what that was,' she said. 'But was that charade really necessary, Inspector?'

'Yes, it was,' he said bluntly.

'But it wasn't an interview. Why did you subject my client to that?' she replied. 'What on earth did you get out of it?'

He smiled. 'You're beginning to sound like one of my constables,' he said. 'Put at its simplest I know that Nancy Collimore didn't kill Keith Connors and we never suspected that she did. I'm satisfied that she wasn't involved in any way. But having announced on national television that we're interviewing suspects in relation to the murder, I had to interview her. And that's exactly what I've done.' The woman frowned and lifted her cigarettes off his table.

'If this continues I'll mention it at my next local police authority meeting,' she warned. 'Interviewing suspects in order to solve crimes is a necessary part of police work. We all accept that. But harassing innocent people so that you can look good on television is entirely unacceptable, Inspector. Don't let it happen again.' Then she slammed his office door and clattered downstairs to catch up with Nancy Collimore.

CHAPTER 24

'I've found somebody who knows about Colombia, sir,' Dalgliesh explained to Inspector Hawthorne. 'He's a visiting fellow at Cambridge University and he's also a research consultant for two American oil companies.'

'What are you waiting for?' Hawthorne replied. 'Show him in!'

Doctor Simmons was tall and thin. His face was drawn in, which gave him a permanently worried look even when he smiled.

'We haven't much time, I'm afraid,' Hawthorne told the academic. 'I need to ask you a difficult question. I'm sorry. In Colombia, do foreign-owned oil companies kill people?'

The academic coughed and winced. 'How do you mean?' he said. 'What are you getting at?'

'At its simplest,' Hawthorne explained, 'everybody knows that the Colombian army devotes entire divisions to guard oilfields. Some people also know that certain units of the Colombian army like the Fourteenth Brigade have an appalling record of human rights violations. What I want to know is: Is there any connection between the killing of innocent civilians in areas like Cartagena, which happens to have an oil refinery in it, and the presence of the foreign oil companies?'

'At its simplest, the answer is yes,' the academic admitted. 'Yes, there is.'

'Explain, please,' the detective instructed.

'Well, they don't really have any choice, you see. It's simply a matter of survival. The oil companies put down infrastructure in Colombia such as the Cano Limon pipeline which runs from the north-eastern Arauca oilfields to the Caribbean port of Covenas. Colombian rebel groups like the ELN guerrillas then blow the infrastructure up. This particular group has sabotaged parts of that pipeline seventeen times this month alone. Sometimes it happens even more frequently than that. So the oil companies are forced to hire militia groups to protect their property and these paramilitary groups massacre and torture civilians. The companies themselves don't tell the militia commanders to do it, obviously. But nevertheless it happens.'

'Are you familiar with these incidents?' Dalgliesh asked.

'Yes, most of them, I suppose,' Simmons replied. 'They happen all the time, so it's difficult to be sure. Why?'

'Could you give us a list? I mean, could you tell us which groups are operating where? Who works for which oil company? And what kinds of incidents have happened in their area?'

'Well, I suppose so,' the academic admitted. 'It would take me some time, but I'm sure it's possible. When would you want me to have it done by?'

'We really are pressed,' Hawthorne explained apologetically. 'It's part of a murder inquiry. Could you have it completed, say, two days from now?'

Joshua Simmons sucked his cheeks in.

'Two days!' he exclaimed. 'Well, it doesn't give me much time. I'll do my best. Don't hold me responsible if there are mistakes in it. Two days isn't anything like long enough, but I'll see what I can do.'

'Well done, Sergeant,' Hawthorne said, after the academic had gone. 'How did you find him?'

'It wasn't difficult at all,' Dalgliesh explained. 'He's staying at the Holiday Inn. Luke Connors told me where to find him. During his academic visit he actually lives in Cambridge and only occasionally travels out here to arrange specialist meetings for Andall Chamber of Commerce. They meet at the local Guildhall on Wednesday nights. Keith Connors was a member, so is his son.'

'That's odd,' Hawthorne said. 'There can't be many oil companies in Andall. What do they do for a whole evening at these meetings of theirs?'

'I don't know, sir,' Dalgliesh admitted. 'Do you want me to find out?'

'Yes please,' the inspector replied. 'But don't spend too long. We've got a murder investigation to conduct. In fact, I tell you what you could do. When you go there, can you get hold of a membership list? It'll give me something to think about when you're off questioning the Andall business elite.'

The minute Dalgliesh left, Hawthorne was back on the phone to the Foreign Office in Whitehall.

'Daniel,' he said when the clerk answered his call. 'It's my turn to ask a favour of you. If I wanted to know more about the foreign-owned oil companies killing the Colombian trades unionists that you were telling me about, who would I ask?' The detective could hear his contact drumming his finger on a table.

'Um, hang on. I'll be back in a minute,' Daniel said.

A few minutes later the Foreign Office clerk picked up the phone again and asked, 'are you there?'

'Yes,' Hawthorne replied.

'There's a BBC journalist called Rob Meeks. He's researching a Panorama programme about Ecopetrol, the Colombian state-owned oil company, and its links to paramilitary violence. He's the person to talk to. I'm sorry I don't have a number for him. Have you got the answer to my question about the meeting yet?'

'No, I haven't,' Hawthorne confessed. 'I'll get it for you before the end of the day. That's a promise.'

It was rash of him to promise an accurate answer to Daniel's question. He simply had no idea whether Ambassador Whittler had met Keith Connors or not and if he had to trace Keith's movements for a whole day to get the answer it would take him longer than he'd promised to find out.

CHAPTER 25

Inside the prison van on a bare metal bench Hilary Connors sat next to her guard with her heart pounding against her rib cage. As they pulled away from the hotel the driver turned to speak to ask him a question. She couldn't understand their conversation, but she caught the repeated name *Abu Sleem* in both the question and its answer. At that precise moment, the name of the most hated and feared prison in the whole of Libya had no reason to mean anything to her. Her guard spoke perfect English and he knew her foreign names. By now, she thought, he must also have been informed about the death of her husband. She pushed her sweating palms together downward, directing her full upper-body weight onto her leg, forcing her left knee to cease its uncontrollable jittering. Her head was pounding. Her words failed, fear had dried her mouth. For the rest of the stifling, humid journey there was silence. Through the grill which separated the driver from his passengers, Hilary saw an endless succession of Colonel Quadaffi's likenesses smiling benignly from the roadside. They slowed at a checkpoint manned by black-bereted soldiers. Lurching over bumps in the road, they passed first a neatly parked succession of military vehicles and then a row of faded, well-used, prefabricated offices and store-rooms. When their bucking, bouncing van stopped abruptly in a swirl of dust, her escort snapped a command to the driver, who turned off the engine and climbed out of the vehicle leaving his door open. Seconds later the glistening steel handles below the shaded, mesh-covered windows began to move, jarring and creaking as they did so. In the instant in which the driver appeared, sheltered, at the open door, she could see one corner of a glass-encased lookout tower embedded in a twenty foot high concrete wall. At the very top, its perimeter was layered with several interlocking courses of razor wire. As she leaned forward to gauge whether they were inside or outside its enclosure, Hilary was blindfolded from behind.

'Out!' her guard ordered as she reached ahead for the nearest support, faltering as she climbed to her feet.

Hilary tried to steady herself by asking, 'what are you bringing me here for?' Her voice crackled, sticking to the back of her throat, and though she knew the meaning of her own question, she couldn't articulate it. She took a breath and felt the floor carefully with her right foot. Without waiting for her to find the exit, the policeman grabbed her armpits and hoisted her forward. While banging the roof with her head, she was propelled into the baking, outside air. Hilary could tell how close she was to the other man by the feel of his garlic breath against her face. And now with her skin burning against the blistering flank of her prison van, she was pressed as her guards secured her feet close together and her hands behind her back.

Ahead of her, as she shuffled, Hilary could hear voices echoing. They sounded long, just like her childhood voice bouncing back from the bottom of a well. In a stone chamber of some kind, a metallic barrier scraped, the garlic breathing driver muttered a curse and called out in Arabic. The voices fell silent. Footsteps approached. A chain rattled and the barrier scraped again.

They moved forward now into a smaller room, where there were no echoes. The room smelt of stale air, urine and sweat. One man held her in the centre of the room while the other took a few paces forward. She could hear him exchanging something made of paper with the stranger. The stranger grunted and cleared his throat. He spat nearby and then a large hand with a damp, soft palm closed round her right arm. For an instant she convulsed involuntarily, in an effort to reach out and stabilise herself. Constrained by her leg chains, she wobbled. Hilary strained and gasped as her light head spun. Once more, she tried to establish the reason for her incarceration. Though she opened her mouth, no words came out; she was breathing too fast. She had to sit down, but she couldn't.

The air became cooler as they passed into a further passage. From somewhere in the distance Hilary could hear voices. The heavy hand shook her arm and she waited. She heard him clink metal on metal and pull open a groaning iron door. On the other side, he undid her blindfold. Momentarily, her painful, compressed eyes clung to their darkness, chasing a series of golden swirls. Muttering, caged voices were all about her now. Not long voices this time. These were dull, surrounded always by the stench of overflowing latrines, densely crowded, unwashed bodies and above all, the cloying scent of fear.

As her private darkness receded, the gaoler pushed Hilary through a final creaking door. This time, however, she was not alone. Before her in a cell almost twenty feet across and an equal depth she

97

estimated there were more than a dozen prisoners, perhaps twice that number. Still chained at the hands and feet, she couldn't manage to avoid dragging her shackles over the shins of the woman curled next to the doorway. But despite the knock, she elicited no response. Clad from head to toe in dirty, faded blue uniforms and without speaking, the prisoners watched her searching for a space.

At first she couldn't understand what was happening. She seemed to be on a concrete floor and someone was putting water on her. When she opened her eyes, she was surrounded by shoulders, pressed in on all sides except her front. Kneeling there was a young woman, about her size, with large, intense, brown eyes staring straight out of deep sockets and embedded in fatigue. Her jet black hair which fell about her shoulders was matted and her prison garb torn. With one hand she dampened Hilary's face, all the while, with the other she kept a small child pressed against her breast.

CHAPTER 26

Hilary had no idea what time it was. She'd been awake for several hours, sitting motionless in the huddle of bodies on the unforgiving, concrete floor. The necessity of remaining still had been her first nocturnal prison lesson. Shivering uncontrollably she'd huddled inside the group, her vibrations spreading like ripples through the dense crush. Then at once, like a piston from nowhere, an elbow thudded into the left side of her face. Following the commotion, Hilary allowed herself to be led to the outside of the huddle. After that, she settled herself a little, in turns, by locking her teeth together and relaxing the whole of her manacled body, as completely as she could, into the rancid, icy air.

Aemilia, with her baby partially hidden in her battered prison uniform, rested peacefully on her shoulder. They had secured a prized section of wall space against which to lean. Though her face still smarted, Hilary didn't yet realise the significance of such security enhancing luxuries as a section of bare wall. Nor did she yet know they were there because she'd already been singled out for the personal attention of their cell leader. Aemilia knew it, but, at the end of her limit of endurance and with her baby asleep, she was too weak and exhausted to invent a method of warning her new-found, foreign friend. In a few cells, nearest the prison entrance, the ones which still had beds, such favoured prisoners slept up above. In the rare cases where mattresses and blankets were available, they had those too. Their acolytes slept close by, sometimes securing for themselves an unused corner of the roughly woven fibres. Even such small advantages were keenly felt during the night when the temperature plummeted. Without exception, all the other prisoners had nothing. Blankets were highly prized. For sport, the guards sometimes gave fresh ones to new arrivals before hurling them into such a communal cell. Then huddled together, against the cell door, they jeered, slapping down bets on how long it would take for the new-comer to be dispossessed and then how long it would take before the shredded remnants of the new blanket found their way to the cell's leader.

Such light-hearted games, however, were only played when the wardens were in high spirits. As Hilary was soon to discover, when their moods were black, they dealt freely in several far more creative forms of sadism. By now, the whole right side of her body was numb. She shifted slightly, sending an agonising spasm from the centre of her waist down into her buttocks. As she clenched her teeth against the immobilising pain, a guard trampled between the cell rows banging his night-stick on the bars. In unison, the other prisoners began to climb to their feet. Hilary tried but couldn't straighten up. Aemilia bent to lift her but with only her left hand, the strain was too great.

'You stand, now! Counting, they counting, now, you stand!' their cell leader hissed. The others crowded at the front of the cell. She was partially hidden. A prisoner took Aemilia's baby, giving her two free hands with which to reach down, but it was too late. The guard turned his key in the door. Standing in the entrance, the fat man counted them quickly. A puzzled look crossed his face and he began again. He stopped counting abruptly, slammed the cell door and hurried away. Hilary could hear voices calling to one another further down the passage. Within minutes a cacophony of boot steps echoed around the prison as a squad of soldiers from the surrounding military barracks approached their cell at the double.

Two other guards appeared before their podgy, flabbergasted cellmaster. In they burst, striking women either side with wooden cudgels. The pair stood either side of Hilary pausing momentarily. Then, together they brought their batons down on her head. The first blow to land found an already weak spot that lingered from an ancient collision with a kitchen cupboard. Screeching in mid-contortion she ducked, as if to dive under her tormentors. At the same time, almost instinctively, she pressed her legs together, but already, a warm, steaming stream had emerged and formed a pool where she sat. Aemilia, to her right, put out her arms to protect her. The intervention served only to make matters worse. Together, by their hair, the women were torn from the cell and dragged towards the prison entrance. In a cell at the end of the passage, she watched them fasten Aemilia to the bed with plastic handcuffs. Though her wrists were red-raw, buckled and bound, her friend did not cry out.

As they were tying her down, a soldier appeared in the doorway. He spoke quickly. They stopped. For a second there was confusion. The guards scattered several open pairs of plastic handcuffs as they ran from the cell. The entire prison complex filled with raised voices.

Then the two women heard several shots followed by screaming. For a moment it seemed to Hilary that the whole prison had been upside down. There was more shouting but from fewer voices, then silence. Hilary shuffled on her knees to the foot of the bed. Against the cell-wall and door-frame she rocked herself to her feet. Aemilia's cut lips were drawn over her teeth. Her face and hair were bloody and where the handcuffs cut into her wrists, her arms were turning purple. There was nothing on the floor which could help her. She had scrabbled about but to no avail. Even in their haste, the guards had locked them in. She leaned over her friend who cried out for the first time as Hilary's weight disturbed her. Taking the cuffs from Aemilia's nearest hand in her mouth, she bit hard.

'I can't do it,' she said, 'I'm sorry it's too hard.' She tried again as her friend's eyes widened. Together they were being quiet as Hilary struggled and Aemilia writhed on the bed. Some time later, Hilary stopped. A tear fell onto Aemilia's grimy face. Hilary watched it and drew a deep breath. Aemilia was silent, she'd be silent too. She was coming apart and she knew it, but she'd keep it all in, nevertheless.

CHAPTER 27

'You don't know me. I'm a detective in Andall,' Hawthorne told the BBC journalist Daniel had informed him about.

'What can I do for you?' Rob Meeks asked.

'Can you tell me simply about the involvement of British oil companies in the deaths of trades unionists in Colombia?' the detective asked.

'Do you only want to know about the deaths of trades unionists?' Meeks said.

'What do you mean?' Hawthorne probed.

'Well, everybody gets killed in Colombia,' Meeks explained. 'You don't have to be a trades unionist to get murdered, raped or kidnapped. All you've got to do is live near an oilfield. People elsewhere get killed too, in large numbers, but the rebels mainly concentrate their presence close to big corporations with lots of money to pay out in ransoms and payoffs for one thing and another.'

'I'm only interested in British companies at the moment,' the detective stressed.

'I'm telling you about British companies,' Rob Meeks replied. 'That's exactly what I'm saying. Oil companies all over Colombia are doing this. It doesn't matter if they're British, American or whoever. It's the only way they can operate. They're basically rebel targets and they've got to fight back. The Colombian government sends its own soldiers to protect the oilfields but mainly those operated by the state-owned oil company Ecopetrol. What's left gets shared around unequally, with the US taking the lion's share of the remaining soldiers. American oil companies get most official protection because America pays by far the most money to the Colombian government in military aid, literally tens of billions of dollars-a-year. We pay only a minute fraction of that amount. So Britain and the other smaller countries like Canada have to make do with what's left over. That's part of the reason why Britain's oil companies have to provide some of their own military protection and they do exactly that.'

'How?' Hawthorne asked.

'Well, they use a range of methods,' Meeks explained. 'Colombia is in the middle of a civil war and there are several sides in the conflict. Firstly you have to distinguish between the paramilitaries and the rebels. They're deadly enemies. By and large the paramilitaries are on the side of the government, the army and the oil companies. If oil companies want to mount a robust defence against rebel attacks, kidnappings and ransoms, they can seek unofficial support from paramilitary groups like the AUC via the Colombian army. The AUC has a particularly nasty reputation. In their last attack on a native village near Tame in North-Eastern Colombia they raped three girls between the ages of eleven and fifteen and then hacked them to death. Then they spent several days slaughtering other villagers. It's become known as the Betoyes Massacre. But that kind of atrocity is typical of them. They deliberately use unspeakably brutal acts on innocent civilians to spread fear. It's a well-organised strategy which benefits foreign investors by pacifying the regions the AUC operates in. To keep the people quiet and to prevent them from harbouring rebel fighters, the militias seek the locals out and slaughter them. The army's reputation is almost as unsavoury but not quite. And then of course there are British security companies who will protect oil pipelines for a fee.'

'Which ones?' Hawthorne asked.

'Well, you probably want to talk to Defence Consultants Limited. They mainly train the local Colombian police force to protect oil installations and pipelines. But the Colombian police force have a reputation which is almost as bad as the army's.'

'When you say security companies, you mean mercenaries, don't you? We're talking about former soldiers from British combat units, aren't we? Let's be clear about this,' Hawthorne said.

'That's right,' Meeks admitted. 'But I wasn't trying to be evasive. That's what they call themselves.'

'You make it sound pretty grim out there,' Hawthorne concluded.

'It is grim,' Rob Meeks warned. 'But it's far worse than I've explained.'

CHAPTER 28

When Hawthorne replaced his telephone handset he was in a state of mild shock. He couldn't clear images of assaulted and butchered children from his mind. He realised that he needed to focus. He needed to know who had killed Keith Connors. It was his primary objective. But his natural revulsion at the things Meeks had revealed to him simply prevented him from doing that.

Hawthorne pressed his index fingers into his temples. He was willing his mind to clear itself. And he was painfully aware of the fact that it would not be possible for him to seek the answers Jarvis sought, on behalf of the Foreign Office, if he continued to operate in a state of such emotional confusion.

In his turmoil Hawthorne saw that between his desk and his office door two brown-skinned adolescents were running. Both were screaming, both were only partly clad. And armed men pursued them determinedly. Hawthorne knew what must necessarily happen next. The fleeing girls would be captured. The rough men would torment them for hours, possibly even for days. And then their wrecked and lifeless bodies would be discarded.

'They're not there,' he said aloud. 'For Christ's sake, they're not there!'

A uniformed constable pushed his head through Hawthorne's doorway.

'I'm sorry, sir? I didn't catch what you said,' the officer explained. 'Who's not where, sir?'

'It's nothing, Andy,' Hawthorne retorted. 'Is the superintendent in? If he's there, tell him that I've gone to interview Simmons again. I'll sort his Foreign Office stuff out as soon as I get back.'

Hawthorne's departure from Andall Road Station was so rapid that he failed even to put his coat on. The young constable in his doorway was almost squashed as he flew past. And he wasn't the only person to be startled by Hawthorne's sudden sense of urgency. Doctor Simmons seemed quite put out by it too.

'I'm sorry to call on you again so soon,' Hawthorne said to Doctor Simmons.

'You said two days, Inspector,' the academic protested. 'It's hardly been two hours! You've come at a bad time. I was just about to go out.'

'I can see that,' the inspector remarked. 'But never mind that now. Can I come in?'

Joshua Simmons retreated into his hotel room, looking even more troubled than usual. The scholar backed into a chair which was laden with writing materials. Everything fell onto his carpet.

As the visiting professor crouched down to retrieve his studies Hawthorne asked, 'what can you tell me about a group of former soldiers who call themselves Defence Consultants Limited?'

'Oh dear,' the academic replied. 'What do you mean?'

'Well, it's a simple question!' the inspector snapped. 'What can you tell me about them? They're hired by British oil companies to protect oil installations from rebel groups in Colombia, aren't they? Do they kill people out there? Do British companies pay British people to go out to Colombia and commit murder? That's what I'm asking. Well, do they or not?'

'Oh,' Joshua replied. 'Oh, right.'

'Well?' the detective insisted.

'Well, yes,' Doctor Simmons said. 'I mean no. Well, it depends on what you mean by murder.'

Hawthorne stared at him.

'It depends on what I mean by murder?' he said. 'I mean killing people with machetes. I mean raping eleven year-old girls and cutting their stomachs open. That's what I mean by murder. What the hell did you think I meant?'

'Oh, that,' Simmons replied. 'They don't do that. Are you speaking about the Betoyes Massacre?'

'Yes, I'm talking about the Betoyes Massacre and the Chengue Massacre and the one at El Salado!'

'Well, they weren't done by British people. They were done by the Colombians themselves.'

'Do British people help in the process?'

'I don't know. It depends on what you mean by help. British people don't give the Peasant Self-Defence of Colombia militia or the paramilitary UAC forces weapons and money and then say, 'go out there and massacre people'. But we do give money to the Colombian army and the army does pass it on to the paramilitaries and they do

105

instruct the militias to kill people. So I guess it just depends on how you look at it.'

'Do you actually know any of the people who work for Defence Consultants Limited?' the detective asked, picking a glossy brochure out of a pile of papers at his feat. 'This looks like promotional material for a private army to me. What is it?'

'Yes, I know one of them,' Doctor Simmons confessed. 'I suppose you already know about the man I'm referring to. He wrote the brochure that's in your hand. He is called Timothy Brydale and the private military company that we are discussing is his. He owns it.'

Hawthorne opened the brochure and read *'Defence Consultants Limited is the world's leading oil security company. Our flagship project is the protection of the Cano Limon Pipeline on behalf of the Colombian government.'*

'When we met you told me that the Cano Limon Pipeline had been blown up more than thirty times,' Hawthorne said. 'How can this company claim that this is a success?'

'You would have to ask them that,' Simmons replied. 'I'm going to see Timothy now. Why don't you come with me?' the academic suggested, pulling his coat on.

Outside Simmons' hotel Andall Road was busier than it had been since the beginning of the fuel strike. Perhaps a third of the shops were still closed. Somebody had made a significant effort to clear away the rubbish sacks. The detective was pleased. The neater streets were a good omen.

Hawthorne smiled. Perhaps he shouldn't have done. It was a momentary lapse in his concentration. The Columbian girls appeared once more. One was cut across her throat from one ear to the other.

'What's the matter?' Simmons asked.

'Nothing,' Hawthorne lied. 'I'm fine.'

'You don't look fine to me,' the academic insisted. 'In fact, you look like a man who has just seen a ghost.'

Inspector Hawthorne cleared his throat and stopped walking.

'Doesn't it bother you?' he asked.

'Doesn't what bother me?' Simmons replied. 'Look, I think we should get going. I'm already late.'

'The Betoyes Massacre, the girls, doesn't it bother you at all?'

'It might, if I thought about it,' Simmons admitted. 'But that's precisely the reason why I don't think about it. I'm an analyst, not a peace campaigner. It's my job to look at the facts, Inspector. People who do my job can't afford the luxury of getting all hung up in the rights and wrongs. Progress costs lives, Inspector. You'd do well to remember that. Now, come along, if you're coming.'

'Where are we going?' Hawthorne said.

'To the airfield,' Simmons replied. 'Brydale has a private plane. I was on my way there about an hour ago when you turned up.'

The two men had reached a line of mesh fencing which ran the entire length of Andall's airfield when Hawthorne finally decided to call his sergeant. At the time he had no instructions to pass on, so he simply relayed his position. The detective stopped under a sign marked, '*Private Land. Keep Out!*' at the entrance to a prefabricated hut. In its doorway there was a stocky man with a crew-cut jeans and a heavy, felt workman's jacket on.

'You're late,' Brydale said to Simmons. 'I've been here for over an hour. Who's this?'

'He's a policeman,' the academic replied. 'He wants to know about Defence Consultants Limited.'

Brydale smiled, standing aside to let his guests into the room. Rows of photographs lined the prefabricated walls. Some were army pictures; men huddled together in battledress with grease-smeared faces and enormous grins. But most of the photographs were of aeroplanes and helicopters. Hawthorne picked an image off the wall which showed Simmons and some now familiar faces standing in front of a helicopter. Across the front of the photograph someone had written in white marker, '*Good luck with the Squirrel - Vince*'.

'Can I keep this picture?' the detective asked. 'I need to speak to this man. Where can I find him?'

'Help yourself,' their host replied. 'He works for me and lives on the Marchant Estate. I've got nothing to hide. When I next see Vince I'll tell him that you want to talk to him, shall I?'

Hawthorne took the photograph and as he left he noticed Brydale lifting his telephone receiver. On his way down the hill the detective looked over his shoulder several times. There was no-one there, and yet, no matter how hard he tried, the detective couldn't shake off the feeling that he was being watched.

CHAPTER 29

Luke put a university prospectus on his father's carpet and answered his phone. Monique poised to interrupt him. He pulled her forward so each of them could hear the conversation.

'Is that Luke Connors?' a clear English voice asked.

'It is, who wants to know?'

'You don't know me, I'm a friend of your mother's. My name is Carter. I'll give you a moment to get a pen and paper, then write this down.' He paused for a few seconds. 'Major Charles E Carter, Intelligence Corps. You'll want look me up no doubt. Your mother needs your help, she could be in grave danger. If I'm right, so could you. Can she count on you?'

'I don't want to seem rude, Major,' he paused, 'Major, er, Carter, but I don't have the faintest idea who you are. How did you get this telephone number anyway?'

'My commanding officer was Colonel Robert Harrison. You'll find him at Defence Intelligence Headquarters Chicksands. I'm sure if you ask him nicely, the colonel will vouch for me. He knows me well, so you can ask them some difficult questions if you like. They'll co-operate with you, I'll make sure he is expecting your call. How you satisfy yourself that I am who I say I am is up to you. I'll call again in twenty four hours. Have a list of questions for me.'

Luke allowed himself a smile. Monique shrugged her shoulders and raised her eyes towards the ceiling.

'Is there anything you want to ask me now?'

Monique shook her head and mimed putting the receiver down.

'Yes,' Luke replied slowly, 'how is my mother?'

'When I last saw her she was fine. She's gone to a safe location somewhere I have no idea of. I specifically asked her not to tell me where she was going. We've had a spot of bother but nothing we couldn't handle.'

'Where are you calling from?'

'At the moment I'm not in England, I'm abroad. But I'm not in the same country as your mother. Was there anything else, before I go?'

'No,' Luke said quietly, 'thanks for calling. If you see my mother, please tell her to come home.'

Monique gathered her cardigan from the floor.

'Moni, wait a minute!' Luke called after her, as she ran from the house leaving the door open. Luke scrambled around to find his keys. By the time he emerged from the house, Monique had vanished.

A policewoman knocked on Hawthorne's door.

'It's Monique Collimore, sir, she's waiting downstairs.'

'Tell her to come up.'

Dalgliesh opened the door to admit the panting girl into the office. 'What's the matter?' he asked, offering her his seat.

'It's Luke,' she replied. 'I think he's in some kind of trouble.'

'What kind of trouble? Where is he?'

'He's at his house. You must come quickly.'

CHAPTER 30

Hawthorne was the first of the detectives to enter Luke's house. He burst through Keith Connors' front door.

'What is it?' he shouted. 'Where's the threat coming from?'

'What threat?' Luke said. 'There's no threat.' Luke was sitting on his father's favourite Persian carpet, in front of a comfortable fire. Although a telephone receiver was in his hand, he was not speaking into it. Sergeant Dalgliesh appeared. He studied the two men in the drawing room and looked upstairs.

'The house is secure,' the sergeant announced. 'Where's the threat?'

'I know where my mum is,' Luke announced.

Simon Hawthorne stared at him, and then at Sergeant Dalgliesh. He then took Luke's telephone receiver and spoke into it. 'Hello?' he said. 'Is anyone there? Hello, hello? Damn it! Sergeant, get a telephone record! For Christ's sake! Oh shit! Luke, who was that on the phone?'

'Someone called Major Carter,' Luke replied. 'I think he said my mum's dead.'

'Dead? What do you mean dead?' Hawthorne probed. 'Dead how, exactly?'

'He said she's been shot,' Luke explained. 'They're in Libya, in a city, and everyone's been shot. They're dead. They're all dead.'

There were now four policemen in the room. A uniformed constable carried a glass of water to the student on the floor. Luke didn't look at the glass. He just took it. With a shaking hand he lifted the glass to his mouth. But instead of drinking, he stared at Hawthorne.

'They're all dead,' he said. 'They're all dead.' With an ever watchful Monique hovering above him, the detective kneeled beside the boy and removed his water glass.

'Come and sit here,' he coaxed. 'Do you want to talk about it?'

'Talk about what?' Luke replied.

'The major,' the inspector explained. 'How did he sound?'

'He was nice,' Luke recalled. 'He was very pleasant. He sounded strong. He wanted to help. That's what he said. He said we should call his headquarters in Bedfordshire. He told me why, but I can't remember.'

'Don't worry. It'll come,' Hawthorne agreed. 'Did he say what type of major he was?'

'He mentioned intelligence,' the student replied. 'Major Charles E Carter, Intelligence Corps.'

'That's good. That's very good!' the detective said. 'Does Major Carter have anyone in mind for us to contact?'

'Oh, yes. Yes of course. Colonel Robert Harrison is in command. That's who we need to speak to.' The student then closed his eyes.

'Is he alright?' Monique asked. 'What should I do?'

'He'll sleep,' the detective predicted. 'He's in shock. When he wakes keep him occupied. If he wants to talk let him. Don't try and stop him talking. Anything we can get out of him will help. Let him talk. Remember anything you can, and if at all possible write what he says down. But don't worry about it. The more concerned we are the more concerned he'll be. It'll work out. Things have a way of working themselves out. You'll see.'

The girl smiled. Maybe she even believed him. While the reassuring words tricked out of his mouth, for a second, Hawthorne believed them himself. But before he'd reached the end of his comforting sentence he was beside himself with rage. He had left Luke's telephone unmonitored, and because of that, the only real lead in Keith's murder case had been squandered. There was no pleasant gloss which could be spread over the situation. It was an unmitigated disaster, and he knew it.

'Stay here!' the inspector barked at two uniformed constables. 'Sergeant, come with me!'

'We weren't to know that a dead man's telephone would be used,' Sergeant Dalgliesh reasoned, a few hours later. 'How did the major know Luke would be in the house anyway?'

'Well, if he knows Hilary, she must have told him,' Hawthorne countered. 'Her son left a message on her answer phone explaining that that's where he was going when he left university. Stopping on the cobblestones in the centre of Saint Anne's Terrace the detective insisted, 'listen! We are on the back foot here. We have got to recover from our mistakes. First I want you to find out all you can about Major Carter. Luke said Bedfordshire, didn't he? He said military intelligence. He might have meant The Ministry of Defence's

Defence Intelligence Headquarters. Their security school is based in Bedfordshire at Chicksands. Perhaps Colonel Harrison belongs there. I want you to do something else for me too, Sergeant,' Hawthorne added.

'Yes, sir. What's that?' Dalgliesh replied.

'We need to issue an Interpol notice for the major, straight away, a red one.'

'Red, sir?' the detective sergeant responded. 'Are we going to arrest him? What for?'

'Assisting a fugitive, Sergeant,' Hawthorne explained. 'It's an arrestable offence common to all of Interpol's member countries. But I'm not finished yet. Prepare Interpol a more gentle notice at the same time, this time a blue one. If we ask for intelligence information on the major we can track him softly too. Let's keep our options open, shall we?'

'I've got an idea too, sir,' Dalgliesh admitted. 'When you were speaking to Luke, I had a detective back at the station contact the consular duty officer at the British Embassy in Tripoli, and told us that there had been a certain amount of unrest, and that for the past few days, gunfire could be heard coming from the outskirts of the city. But he said, details about exactly who had been shooting at whom, had been difficult to come by. And, sir, I've got more bad news.'

'Is there more?' Hawthorne asked.

'Yes, sir, I'm afraid there is. The duty officer thinks that Major Carter was part of a trade delegation, sir. That trade delegation included Ambassador Whittler at the time when he was murdered. The Americans are desperate to speak to Carter about Whittler's murder, but they can't find him, sir. Apparently he hasn't been seen since Ambassador Whittler was killed, and nobody knows where he is. At least they didn't know where he was until he called Luke here. I think Luke Connors was confused when he said they're all dead. The security situation is very unclear. It's not his fault. There have been many deaths. The reports I've heard are confusing, but I think the Libyan police and security services are actually the ones doing the killing. The duty officer said there were a number of conflicting rumours circulating. The Libyan Interior Ministry has issued one report claiming that the explosions and gunfire, which have been heard for days now, have an innocent explanation. They said in a statement that soldiers at a military barracks adjacent to Tripoli's main prison, Abu Sleem gaol, have destroyed a large stockpile of degraded munitions. Nobody has been killed, and that reports of gunfire emanating from within the city, are mistaken. It's a lie, though, sir, a government cover-up. The consular duty officer also heard about eye-witness accounts from prisoners at Abu Sleem gaol, who saw a large number of inmates being executed by firing squads. He says these accounts are the ones everyone in Tripoli is listening to. According to these statements, the bodies are being transported out of the prison in a succession of refrigerated lorries and dumped outside the city. But I've got an idea. Why don't we put out an urgent appeal for Hilary Connors on the BBC World Service? We can say she needs to contact her son urgently. By doing that we can bypass the Libyan police and security services altogether, sir. As time goes by we can repeat our appeals to the British Embassy Consulate Section for a clearer view, through the consul, of what the hell's been going on over there. We need to know what's going on, not just for Hilary, but for everybody.'

'You have been busy!' Hawthorne remarked. 'It's an excellent plan. Let's do it,' he said. 'Oh, and Sergeant?'

'Yes?' Dalgliesh replied. Hawthorne smiled and resumed his journey.

'Thank you,' he said.

CHAPTER 31

Hilary Connors had her face pressed against Aemilia's when the gateway to their cell rattled for the first time. Though she opened one eye in response to the sound of grating steel, she did not look up. If she had she would have seen a familiar prisoner from their previous cell struggling to unlock their door. Their saviour hissed an alert which Aemilia acknowledged by lifting her head a fraction above her blood-stained mattress. Within seconds, there were several women in the room. As she turned slowly, on her knees, to shield her friend's body with her own, the scarred face of Hilary's earlier assailant loomed overhead, casting her in shadow. She should have moved to allow the newcomers a closer view of Aemilia's shackles, since they clearly constituted a rescue party. Instead, she was transfixed. Suddenly, her vivid memories of the elbow which had smashed into her face paralysed her. She knew she was shaking because her manacles rattled. Even when she pressed her hands together, she couldn't make them stop. Their faces were very close to hers now, and their mouths moved. Her eyes followed the group leader's tongue as it flickered across her teeth. Hilary tried to focus on the words, but of the garbled clutter that reached her ears, nothing made sense.

Chiselling with crude implements while one held her mouth closed, the women freed Aemelia from the bed. Two rescuers bundled them from the cell. Every door in their prison block was open and all the cells were empty. Torn, dirty prison uniforms, ripped scraps of paper and bedding lay strewn in cell doorways and along the halls. Endless shouts from every direction reverberated off the solid concrete walls like storm thunder closing in on an exposed mountaineer. The prisoners had gathered in three groups, the largest of which clustered around the entrance to the cell block.

Another group had climbed through a breech in a dividing wall into the men's prison. Hilary's small group were too far away to see what was happening and the hole was partially obscured by a cloud of dust. All those who remained, however, could hear long, piercing screams coming from that direction. A third, much smaller group, a few feet from where they emerged, were arguing about how to break into the last secure cell. This one belonged to sixty prisoners known as the Werfalla group. It was the only cell in the complex, whose locks could not be broken.

Their cell leader and two members of the Werfalla rescue party set about releasing Hilary from her shackles. They succeeded as several shots rang out. The shooting came from two sides of an outside quadrangle. The majority of the women prisoners had gathered near a damaged wall which divided the woman's prison from the men's. A large number of panicked prisoners ran through their tiny group. Hilary and their cell leader were pushed along the passage by the crush. Realising that Aemilia was not with them, she shouted and grabbed her companion's arm. In an entrance to a passageway where they paused to gather breath, they heard the diminutive cry of a tiny child. Aemelia and a stranger holding a small bundle of prison clothing crouched behind them in the gloom.

'We go,' her companion, the cell leader, hissed, 'we go!'

'Look at these!' Hilary protested, drawing their attention to Aemilia's wrists.

'You hold!' the leader replied, pushing Hilary's hand over her friend's mouth. Then raising the restrained woman's right wrist against the wall, she aimed her crude chisel. Several strikes later the plastic cuff crumpled away. Hilary did her best to muffle Aemilia's cries. Together, they replaced Aemelia's freed arm with her other. The exhausted woman slumped to the ground.

'We go!' the cell leader hissed. Supporting the unconscious woman between them, they continued down the passageway, feeling their way as they went.

At some distance from the entrance to the passage, they came into an underground vault. A small amount of light pierced the chamber from a flue high above. They rested. From outside they could hear the sound of lorries manoeuvring, then shouting. There were several seconds of silence followed by more shouting and then a volley of gunfire. This pattern was repeated for a considerable length of time. Pulling herself into the vent and digging into the crumbling wall with her improvised chisel, the cell leader began to climb. Some time later, she scrambled back to the ground and grabbed Hilary's shoulders.

'You look!' she instructed.

Hilary took the sharp metal object and with great difficulty she clambered to the top of the shaft.

Outside the prison, in a different part of the compound, the male prisoners were lined up. Before them in rows with their profiles towards Hilary a line of soldiers stood. She watched them take aim. Everybody stood still. The youngest soldier nearest to her vantage point fidgeted. She watched him wipe his brow with the back of his hand. They fired. The prisoners fell to the ground. A second later, the young soldier fired at an empty space in the wall and then wheeled and vomited on his boots. A high-sided lorry which was turning, stopped abruptly. She could see two rows of hands gripping the tailgate from the inside. Suddenly, as the vehicle started forward, the cab door opened and its driver jumped to the ground. The officer in charge of the execution detail strode across the yard. Hilary watched him take two hand-grenades from the young soldier, now standing to attention a few paces behind the others. He made no reaction at all when his commander approached him. He seemed not to realise the officer was there. Even from where she was, Hilary could see that the boy in uniform was petrified.

The commander pushed his peaked cap to the back of his head and studied the two grenades by turning them over slowly, as he walked towards the rear of the lorry. Wiping his nose with his left hand, he withdrew the pin from the first grenade and straightened his tunic. Then, tipping his hat back over his forehead, he pitched the activated hand-grenade into the rear of the truck.

CHAPTER 32

Involuntarily, Hilary clutched the grate as she recoiled from the explosion. She slipped, and momentarily thrashed about for a foothold while dangling in mid-air. Spitting and blinking with her face chafing against the rough masonry, she attempted to remove a particle of dirt from her eye. More falling debris rained down as she dislodged the iron guard, from which she was suspended. The chorus of shouts, from both inside and outside the prison had ceased. There were no sounds at all. She lifted her eyes level with the grate. Outside, a soldier, who was tilting backwards, shuffled as he dragged a limp corpse across the compound. The dead man's trailing arms cut tracks into the dust. In the final stage of his macabre duty, the young conscript turned in her direction. Hilary released the railing and fell part of the way down the shaft. The group leader clutched her shoulders, shaking her back to the present.

'Come, you, we make the big hole.' She pointed upwards and began to scale the wall. Hilary's heart lurched against her chest.

'It's not safe,' she pleaded.

The woman on the wall twisted and raised her voice, 'they kill all, you, you, all. We go, safe, not safe, we go!' She shifted to improve her grip, before adding, 'you give the...' bereft of the correct vocabulary, she mimed a striking motion.

Voices sounded above the opening and a cluster of dust plummeted down the shaft. The climber froze. Hilary stopped breathing. Very slowly and quietly, the leader returned to the ground. And then they stood without moving or speaking. The fourth prisoner broke the grotesque silence, speaking in Arabic. They hushed her in unison. Then engines sounded, at first distinct vehicles could be heard. Then more, until the din became a grinding mass of noise.

The cell leader squatted inches from where she sat. 'We make hole, you, you. We make the hole, yes?'

It was the first time inside the prison Hilary had felt that her opinion was being sought, but there it was. Somehow she would respond, even though she had nothing to offer. She hadn't any idea where they were. Their situation was desperate, that much was already obvious to all of them. Even if she had known what to do, she wouldn't have been able to share her ideas. One thing she did know though, was if they were to escape through the vent, they'd need some method of pulling Aemelia and the baby up after them. With her hands and wrists badly cut and bruised, she would never make it through the wall on her own.

She positioned Aemelia beneath the shaft, miming the act of harnessing her friend and pulling up a heavy weight.

The leader tapped her shoulder, 'pull, heh? Pull.'

Hilary nodded, and added under her breath, 'and for that, we need rope.'

'You come.'

Together, they re-entered the passage leading towards main prison. Every few steps they stopped and listened. For the length of the dark, slimy passage, their nostrils filled with the odour of decay. Crouching beneath the low ceiling in the final ante-chamber, they stopped. The sounds of the prison were clear here. She could hear something scraping across a concrete floor. They waited. As Hilary dithered, her companion pushed past through the narrow opening. Her attempt to follow was impeded by an oncoming bundle. She gathered an armful of blankets and reversed to make way, as the other woman twisted back into the tunnel. They descended again into the vault, this time faster. Her companion began to tear the blankets into strips, binding them together. As the remaining daylight faded, Hilary scaled the flue and began to cut away the wall. In time, she had a hole large enough for each of them to pass through. They had to decide how they were going to make their escape. There were two realistic options: either they all went together, or somebody reconnoitred first. Whoever did that would have to explain what she saw and that wasn't going to be easy. She removed the grating and lowered it down to the floor. The fourth prisoner, who had fastened the sleeping child to her shoulders, tied Aemelia to their makeshift harness. Kneeling with her hands clasped, Hilary began to recite the Lord's Prayer. She sensed the others settling close around. To her, their soft recitations were unintelligible. But regardless of its form, the significance of each appeal was lost on no-one.

CHAPTER 33

'Please listen carefully, everybody,' Detective Inspector Hawthorne said to a group of assembled officers, at his station in Andall Road. 'I want to explain Operation Extract to you. We've had a scenario like this planned even before the fuel crisis began. It involves hundreds of officers and will not be co-ordinated by us. Gold Command for this operation will be located in the operations room at Easley Main Station, so let me explain. We know who attacked Luke Connors late on Thursday evening in his father's house. His name is Vincent Hanner. The student was attacked by three people. We think we know who the others are. We also think that the motive for attacking Luke was related to the reason why his father was murdered but we don't know what it was. Hanner is an employee of Timothy Brydale's and Brydale is a director of the firm Defence Consultants Limited. That's a private military company and it's perfectly legal in this country.'

One of the room's uniformed officers laughed and asked, 'private military company, sir, doesn't that mean he's a mercenary?'

'Yes, and no, Barton, is the answer,' Hawthorne told him. 'Technically, a person who fights is a mercenary. Private military companies often get round this matter, if getting round is the right way to look at it, by simply not fighting. They pay other people to do the fighting on their behalf, and just sell their military, or technical, expertise instead.'

Then Sergeant Dalgliesh stepped forward. 'I need volunteers,' he said. 'We need to arrest Hanner. We don't think he was involved in the physical murder of Keith Connors but as the inspector has just said, he did assault Keith's son Luke. And we think he knows why Keith died. We know that he's dangerous, obviously. Given the circumstances, a little of his military background is relevant to the operation. Hanner was a sergeant in the Royal Marines for nine years and he's served two tours of duty in Northern Ireland. He was discharged last year. We'll have an armed response unit backing us up

119

on the arrest. But as far as we know Hanner is not armed. Volunteers please?'

At first none of the men present responded. Then Constable Barton chipped in again. Within seconds enough of his colleagues had been recruited and the operation began to get underway.

'We've already got a problem, sir,' Sergeant Dalgliesh informed Hawthorne as he tried to collect his officers together. 'Vincent Hanner has gone onto the Marchant Estates. We can't follow him into the housing development because it's too dangerous.'

'We can't just leave him there either,' Hawthorne replied angrily. 'Police work doesn't stop just because a suspect lives in a rough neighbourhood, Sergeant. That's what Operation Extract was designed specifically to deal with. If Hanner has gone into the Marchant then we'll just have to go in there and bring him out again, won't we?'

'I know Easley Main Station has been planning the Operation Extract scenario for quite some time, but implementing it is going to be impossible,' Dalgliesh complained. 'When we started planning, we had no idea how bad the fuel shortages were going to get. We've used up all our fuel reserves. We don't have any vehicles because we've no petrol and we can't get reinforcements to the area because we've no vehicles. We can't get a helicopter into the sky above the area because our police air reconnaissance unit has got no fuel either and we can't take mounted riot police in between the buildings because protesters can throw missiles at them from the rooftops. And we've no fuel to drive a water cannon in to protect the horses from attack with. It's hopeless, sir. It's impossible. It can't be done.'

'We can get horses and men onto the wasteland outside the housing estate, can't we, Sergeant?' Hawthorne asked.

'Yes, sir,' Dalgliesh admitted. 'But there's no danger on the wasteland. It's too far away from the houses. Why would you want to put riot police out there?'

'To look menacing, Sergeant,' Hawthorne said. 'How many men can we muster in full riot gear by mid afternoon?'

'About two hundred. Maybe we could get fifty more from another station. Is that enough?'

'It'll have to be,' Hawthorne said, shrugging his shoulders. The inspector was worried. He made an effort not to show his men. He had a real problem. Nobody knew how long the country would have to last without petrol. Policing had to be done, fuel or no. The question he had to face was: Should he postpone his foray into the

Marchant and hope that his force could be resupplied? Or should he operate with his existing constraints? He knew the answer. He'd always known the answer. He didn't want to expose his officers to any risk and he had to do exactly that.

'Easley Main Station has agreed to send us all of the officers they can spare,' Dalgliesh informed his inspector. 'We'll have almost four hundred men in total. They're sending us their silver commanders, two superintendents and a chief superintendent to oversee the operation too, sir.'

'Remember to keep out of sight,' Hawthorne instructed. 'We don't want to inflame the situation by appearing to be confrontational.' With a small army of men behind him, all wearing blue steel helmets and holding transparent, Perspex riot-shields, Hawthorne approached the crack dealing dens on the outskirts of the Marchant Estate.

Outside Mandela House, the first high-rise block of flats, which was nearest to the waste ground the policemen had just crossed, two young boys were playing football. The boys ignored the detective. They continued, ignoring Hawthorne, until the first riot shield came into view behind him. Then they stopped and stared. The detective knew he had to move quickly. The block of flats he was heading for was in the middle of the estate. He and his men would be cut off and isolated when they reached it. If they moved quickly perhaps they could still return through a peaceful housing complex. The men had just formed a line behind a vehicle with smashed front and rear windows when six youths appeared on a balcony above them. Hawthorne pointed to the flat where Vincent was. It was a hundred meters from where they stood. More youths appeared both around Mandela House, which was now behind them and in Victoria House towards which they were heading. Several of the young men were speaking into mobile phones. It was clear to Hawthorne that they were mustering, so he urged his men on.

CHAPTER 34

On the second level of the high-rise block of flats called Victoria House, Vincent Hanner opened his front door. In front of him there was a black detective with his identity card in plain view and behind the detective two policemen in full riot gear.

'Vincent Hanner, I'm arresting you on suspicion of having committed an act of grievous bodily harm,' the detective said. 'You do not have to say anything. But it may harm your defence if you do not mention when questioned something which you later rely on in court. Anything you do say may be given in evidence.'

Hanner, a squat, tough looking man with thin eyes and closely cropped hair, hardly reacted at all. He looked neither surprised nor upset and even placed his wrists together in front of the detective for him to handcuff. As Hawthorne clicked his cuffs in place he noticed a diamond-shaped scar above Hanner's left elbow. The men then moved towards the concrete stairwell which Hawthorne and his officers had just climbed. There were two young men in bright tracksuits below. Neither of them looked older than eighteen.

'Move back!' Hawthorne instructed, climbing down towards them. The youths started to retreat, turned a corner and ran. Hawthorne descended. On the next landing there were several youngsters. On the one below that there were even more still.

A stone flew past the detective's face. It struck a wall and clattered to the floor. The stone-thrower shouted, 'I hate fucking coons!'

Hawthorne recognised both the voice and its message. He'd heard the same youth saying precisely that, in almost exactly the same place a few days earlier. He knew who the voice belonged to. Another stone struck the wall. He radioed to Dalgliesh.

'Bring about a hundred men into the east entrance to the estate,' he said. 'And do it quickly!'

Two policemen on chestnut-coloured horses with their Perspex visors closed and their batons drawn appeared at the corner of Mandela House.

'Go down!' Hawthorne said.

He and the men descended. At the foot of Victoria House, a few yards away from the car with smashed windows, Hawthorne and his men regrouped. There were now male residents, of all ages, on every balcony in the housing complex. There were hundreds of them, maybe thousands. In every direction Hawthorne could see nothing except a sea of screaming faces, shouting 'wugh, wugh wugh!' again and again. He was deafened. A bottle smashed at his feet. Where Hawthorne and his men stood there was no protective cover. An open space two hundred meters long stretched between them and safety. A line of police horses stood in the housing estate exit, next to Mandela House. Hawthorne led his men forward. A crowd from each of the buildings in front swarmed down to cut them off. Screaming men and boys poured out onto the street on all sides. Some were waving sticks, others clubs. Some held in their hands anything they could find. Behind a wall of transparent shields Hawthorne, his prisoner and his men moved forward.

'They're on all sides of us, sir,' a battle-clad policeman told the inspector. 'The horses coming in are pushing the crowds towards us, not away.'

A brick crashed into the shield protecting Hawthorne's face. Another smashed into Hanner's unprotected legs. He stumbled. Hawthorne pulled him up.

'I'm alright!' the captive grunted. 'Let go of me, for fuck's sake!'

Two rows of black-clad policemen on horseback charged into the crowd. The mêlée split in half. While the horses at the centre of the onslaught advanced, those on its flanks wheeled. Two perfectly straight lines of mounted riders, one on each side of the approaching equestrian rescue party, lashed out at the Marchant men below them.

CHAPTER 35

'I've come from a debriefing by the Chief Constable on Operation Extract. Your contribution was noted. Well done, Inspector,' Superintendent Jarvis called up from the foyer of Andall Road Police Station. 'And I also heard from Chief Superintendent Trent, Operation Extract's silver commander, how you arrested the man who attacked the Connors boy. We need to talk about him.'

'I can't discuss it,' the detective explained. 'I've got to receive a telephone call from overseas. We think we know where Hilary Connors is, sir. We think we're at least part of the way to tracking her down.'

'Tracking her down where?' the fat superintendent insisted. 'Where the hell is overseas? And regardless of where it is, how on earth did she get there?'

'I really have to go, sir. The prisoner is in cell two,' Hawthorne said, putting on his coat.

Dalgliesh, together with a man in workman's clothes, was waiting for the inspector in the police station car park.

'This is Stebson from criminal intelligence, sir,' the sergeant said. 'I've taken him from Operation Extract without permission. There simply wasn't time to go through the proper channels.'

Hawthorne nodded and imagined how rapidly his approval rating with the high command at Easley Main Station would evaporate when they learned that he was commandeering their specialist staff without authorisation. In any event, it was too late to do anything about it now.

'He is actually a telephone engineer by trade,' Dalgliesh explained. 'Or rather he was.' The three men set off, westwards, in the direction of Keith Connors' house, on foot.

'Because we've arrived late, I doubt there will be time to tap the victim's phone in advance,' Hawthorne explained to the engineer. 'If you add a recording device to his telephone circuit while I'm talking to the suspect, will the man at the other end hear you?'

'He might do,' the telephone specialist admitted. 'The line might go completely dead or make a clicking sound. If your man is switched on enough he shouldn't have any trouble working out what we're up to. I'd rather my job was completely finished before the conversation starts, if it's possible.'

Outside Keith's house in Saint Anne's Terrace the specialist approached a green metal cabinet tucked beneath a lamppost at the edge the pavement. He opened the steel cupboard, and as the detectives watched, he set to work among the cables inside.

'OK, it's all ready,' he said, seconds later. The inspector knocked on Luke's door and Monique let the trio inside.

'Would anyone like a cup of tea?' she offered as they filed into Keith's ornate hallway. Hawthorne was about to reply when the phone rang. Everybody remained motionless, as for several seconds the phone's harsh ring filled the house. It took what seemed like an age for the inspector to pick the receiver up.

'Detective Inspector Simon Hawthorne, Suffolk CID,' he said. For quite some time Simon Hawthorne received no reply.

'I want to speak to Luke Connors,' Major Carter said.

'I know you do, and you can,' Hawthorne explained. 'I've got a proposal for you.'

'For me?' Major Carter replied in a jittery voice. 'How can you have a proposal for me? You don't even know who I am.'

'We checked your credentials with The Defence Intelligence and Security Centre at Chicksands, just as you knew we would. You must have been expecting us to be here. You're in trouble, Major Carter, and you know it. The Americans won't be nearly as accommodating as we're prepared to be. They don't yet know exactly what happened to Ambassador Whittler, but it won't take them long to work it out. They already know that Whittler arranged to meet Keith Connors. They haven't pieced together what went on between the two men. They want my help to do that. I've procrastinated and delayed for as long as I can, but they'll work out the truth with or without my help within a day or two. Then they'll know how Hilary was involved. And when they know that, they'll find you. So let's get straight down to business, shall we? You haven't got much time.'

'I'm listening, Inspector. How can you help me?' the major said.

'First,' Hawthorne replied, 'I need to know where Hilary Connors is.'

'I can't tell you that, Inspector,' Major Carter explained. 'She's gone.'

125

'What do you mean, gone?' the detective insisted. 'Gone where?'

'I don't know,' said Carter. 'That's what I mean. She simply vanished. Somebody took her from her hotel.'

'Major, you're not making much sense,' Hawthorne warned. 'Why don't you start from the beginning?'

'I met her in Tripoli, about a week ago. Her husband had just been murdered and she thought his accountant, Christopher Delatouche, might have been involved, somehow.'

The telephone engineer raised his wristwatch into the air and mouthed silent signals at the detective, who nodded.

'Go on,' Hawthorne said. 'Who took her from her hotel?'

'This phone signal is coming from Geneva,' the engineer hissed. 'He's somewhere near the lake, but I can't tell you where.' As he spoke, police sirens sounded in the distance behind the major.

'You've followed my phone signal,' he said. 'Look, I've got to go. It was an American who killed the ambassador, not one of us. I don't know why Whittler was killed, but I do know that his death had nothing to do with Hilary Connors.'

CHAPTER 36

'Tripoli?' Superintendent Jarvis roared. 'What the hell is Hilary Connors doing in Tripoli, for Christ's sake? And how the hell did she get there, anyway?'

'We don't know, sir,' Hawthorne admitted. 'Apparently she went there to meet someone called Major Carter. He contacted Luke. That's how we know about him.' Jarvis' eyes narrowed.

'Tripoli, that's where the American politician was killed, isn't it?' he said. 'He had a meeting with Connors, didn't he? Not the wife but the husband. Where's the telephone number of that Foreign Office clerk? I think I've got something for him! By Jove, I think I've got something!'

'Before you get too excited, sir, we're not out of the woods yet. The woman's been taken from her hotel.'

'Taken from her hotel?' Jarvis repeated. 'Taken by whom? Taken where, for God's sake?'

'We never found that out,' Hawthorne confessed. 'We alerted the police in Geneva when we traced the major's phone call but he'd absconded by the time they arrived.'

'Don't tell me it gets worse,' Jarvis flustered. 'What phone call?'

Hawthorne wasn't listening. He'd already left the superintendent's office. Within minutes he and Dalgliesh were facing Vincent Hanner in an austere police interview room, over a plain tabletop.

'You have a right to have a solicitor present,' Hawthorne told Hanner. 'You know that.'

'I don't want one,' the military man replied. 'I don't need one.'

'OK, so why did you break into Keith Connors' house, steal his drawings and attack his son?' Dalgliesh asked.

'We didn't break in. We used a key and in any case the drawings weren't his. They were ours. Beating up Luke was a mistake. I admit that. If you want me to apologise to him, I'll apologise. I don't have a problem with that. If you want to charge me, charge me. I admit it. I beat him up. I'm sorry.'

'For the benefit of the tape, the interview terminated at eleven o-five,' Hawthorne declared. The two detectives paused outside the interview room door.

'This is a ploy,' Dalgliesh concluded. 'Hanner is shielding Timothy Brydale and the Defence Consultants Limited directors from something, but from what? They didn't murder Luke's father.'

'He came in too easily on the Marchant,' Hawthorne agreed. 'You weren't there, of course. But I could have sworn he was helping us to arrest him and now he's preparing his own charge. You're right, Sergeant. There's something wrong here.'

'He knows you've got his fingerprints from the photograph in Brydale's office,' Dalgliesh reasoned. 'Maybe he's just doing the sensible thing in confessing.'

'We need to trip him up,' Hawthorne declared. 'He's got no criminal record. This is his first offence. He's served Britain honourably as a soldier. It'll work in his favour with the magistrate. If he's unlucky, he'll get a suspended sentence on top of a fine. Most likely he'll just get the sentence. This isn't about the attack on Luke Connors, Sergeant. Whatever it is that Doctor Simmons is advising Brydale and Hanner to do, it has absolutely nothing to do with Luke. He was simply in the wrong place at the wrong time. I'm sure of it. When the men said 'stay out of what doesn't concern you' to the student, they actually meant it quite literally.'

'Were the other two men who attacked Luke Brydale and Simmons then, sir?' Dalgliesh asked in surprise. 'Luke Connors knows Joshua Simmons from the chamber of commerce. If Luke knew it was Simmons who called out in an American accent during the assault, then why didn't he say so?'

'What exactly is your role in Brydale's private military company?' Hawthorne asked Hanner as soon as he got back into the interview room.

'I'm not answering any questions,' Vincent Hanner said. 'I admit that I hit the boy. I'll sign a statement, but that's it. I'm not answering any questions.'

'We're stuck then, sir,' Sergeant Dalgliesh concluded as the detectives made their way back upstairs.

'No we're not!' the inspector replied. 'We're far from stuck. Why did Brydale have a key to Keith Connors' house? What sort of drawings would he have, anyway? He's a soldier not an engineer. And why would Connors have schematics which didn't belong to him?'

CHAPTER 37

After the prayers, in their tiny dungeon, Hilary kept her mind blank and her body moving. She checked Aemelia's harness and the sleeping child. As she bent down, the fourth prisoner clutched her hands. For a second, the crouching woman's shroud of uncertainty and fear enveloped them both. Hilary dispelled her overwhelming urge to retreat. And instead, in the darkness, she placed her hand on the young woman's trembling shoulder. She decided not to speak, guessing that her quavering voice would betray her own fears. Behind them, Tibra, the group leader, ventured up to the grating for a final check. She returned to shake Hilary's clothing in a agitated manner, 'sound, clack?' she repeated. Hilary was temporarily confused. 'My pockets,' she began, more in a spirit of co-operation than comprehension. And then it dawned on her, Tibra was asking if any of her possessions rattled. She turned out her pockets obediently. She had nothing but a small fold of paper. Even in the gloom, she could still make out the major's rapid scrawl. She folded it again, carefully and buttoned it inside her torn blouse.

The courtyard was now completely silent. Between them, the women had cut away several inches of rough mortar. The hole around the grate was now some twenty inches wide and a similar height. For over three hours they waited, until, with almost exaggerated care, Tibra pulled the loose grating and lowered it. She took a blanket and pushed one end out into the courtyard. Nothing happened. She waived the blanket gently, and then increasingly vigorously. Following a brief period of inactivity, she began to widen the space around the hole. Tibra then waved the blanket once more, and waited. After several pauses, she pushed her left arm out into the courtyard. She began to descend, pulling Hilary towards her as she stepped onto the ground, 'now, we go, you out!'

Hilary's left knee jittered. It had bashed against the sharp, stone wall twice during her present ascent. She ground her teeth together. Her fingers refused to grip individually and she pulled herself up by bunching them together. The climb hurt this time. Everything strained. She exhaled. I have to remember to breathe! she reminded herself. Something rattled in front of the hole. She froze, pressing herself against the stonework. A scrap of paper twisted across the yard.

'Come on, you can do this,' she whispered, brushing her lips against the wall. 'It's only a piece of paper. You have to keep moving.' Eventually, she pushed her head through the narrow opening. The deserted courtyard was moonlit. To her left and at almost right angles from the cellar in which they were confined, there was a double gate in the outer wall. Between it and her, three empty vehicles stood: The first, a refrigerated trailer with its rear doors open; the second, a tall-sided, short-wheel-based truck, leaning awkwardly to one side; and the third, a battered, green Unimog, with eight shovels resting against its tailgate. At irregular intervals between the vehicles clumps of debris had been scraped together. Shovel marks in the dust converged towards the centre of each pile. In the middle of the nearest shovel track, glinting in the half-light, Hilary could make out a small booklet. Its pages and torn cover flapped in the easterly breeze, towards the gate. Poised halfway between a stoop and a crouch, she scanned the cell block roof-top. Then, she pulled Tibra's emerging arms. Together, they moved swiftly along the south west compound wall, where the darkness was greatest. Halfway as they turned towards the gate, the women were met by gust of wind, pregnant with the stench of intestines.

Hilary reached the truck first and ducked beneath it. Following a brief pause, they darted to the side of the trailer and pressed themselves along its flank as far as they could. There was now a gap of approximately twenty feet between them and the gate. Through the corner of her blouse, Hilary took a deep breath. She listened. There were voices and engines too, but they were all some way off. She ran and pressed her whole body flat against the left gatepost. Now she was sure, the gate and its gatepost were not aligned, nor had they been fastened together. The women doubled back in stages. Between them they pulled Aemelia into the courtyard. Hilary leant inside the shaft to bring the baby out first. The fourth prisoner and the blankets followed.

Tibra led the tiny party underneath the truck, retrieving an army jacket from a pile of refuse on the way. It stank. Its previous owner, Hilary felt sure, had been the queasy recruit. They climbed aboard the smallest lorry and lay flat. Tibra covered them with blankets stacked the shovels and raised the tailgate. Then, wiping down the jacket, she started the Unimog and pulled out of the compound. She waited with her engine and lights off, until, from the right, another lorry followed by a jeep turned towards the main compound gatehouse. Tibra fell in behind them. A black beretted guard stepped in front of the lead vehicle as they pulled up to his checkpoint. Behind him on the other side, the barrier raised to admit more jeeps and a long procession of articulated lorries. The lead driver flashed his headlights and sounded his air horn to clear the road. Waiving both arms at the agitated, incoming truck-driver, the soldier jumped onto the verge to allow the women through.

CHAPTER 38

For some time the lorry remained stationary. Hilary lay on her side with the child clutched to her chest. Aemelia faced toward her. The fourth prisoner, curled in the top right corner, balanced her open palm on Hilary's shoulder to prevent her from rolling forward. When the engine started, the hand gripped her shoulder. Tibra revved the engine and the rear of the truck was filled with exhaust fumes. Simultaneously she and the prisoner, against whom she lent, began to fan the air around the child. They rolled forward slowly. Hilary guessed they had moved about two hundred metres. Then they stopped. They could hear engines all around them, then voices. There were footsteps, more voices and suddenly a series of loud horn bursts. Many more engines started up. Just as the crescendo of engine noises seemed to become overwhelming, they lurched forward. The front of their vehicle bumped a second before they did. Aemelia cried out. The hand on Hilary's shoulder vanished and the succession of later bumps was met with silence. They turned left. The road was smooth. They'd picked up speed. Hilary followed the first few turns. They'd reached a roundabout and were now on a long straight road. Their speed increased again. Hilary was the first to sit up. The others followed. In turns they guided Aemelia towards the panel which separated them from the cab.

Her back had locked into position. Hilary ignored its dull ache, by concentrating instead on the flickering canvas flap hanging over the tailgate. Whenever the jittering lorry disturbed it, the flap let in the tiniest sliver of light. Tibra slowed and crunched through the gears. They were bumping on an uneven surface and then tipping downhill. Very slowly and methodically they began to turn in all directions. Then without warning, they stopped.

Tibra, holding a lantern, raised the flap. She spoke in Arabic. They were in some kind of underground chamber. Its red, sandstone walls were high. There were two tunnels leading into the cavity. As the lantern moved, Hilary could see yet more tunnels joining those in front of her. The driver paced back and forth while the others tended to the mother and child.

And finally she said, 'you come!'

'But we can't just leave the others in the dark!' Hilary protested in vain. Tibra was already rounding the first corner ahead. As the inky blackness enveloped them, Hilary began to run.

'This Gharyan, all person know Gharyan, soldiers come. All person know Gharyan, tourist come,' her guide urged, breaking into a trot.

Moving at the speed of the woman in front, Hilary wound her way through the warren of interconnecting passages and chambers. At the bottom of a passage slightly narrower than the others, Tibra dropped to her knees and began to search for something. As Tibra scraped away the accumulated dust, Hilary noticed an irregularity in the structure of the floor. Ignoring Hilary completely, Tibra worked, until a tiny crack appeared. And later, having spent much energy struggling fruitlessly, her guide instructed her to remain, and returned up the passage. After a considerable period of time, Hilary climbed to her feet and felt her way to the first fork in the tunnel. She knew Tibra and her lantern had turned right. But she didn't know which direction she had taken after that. She tried the right passage first. In total darkness, Hilary crawled along each passageway, making a small mound of dust inside each corner as she went, to guide her, should she return. When she was no longer sure exactly how many turns she'd made, she began to work backwards. At the end of the narrower passage, Hilary lowered herself to the ground. She whispered to the wall, 'I'll give her another hour'. Then she tapped both sides of her head, to disrupt her recurring images of Katherine Clifton dying slowly in the film *The English Patient*. But, unlike Katherine, she knew she was in a commonly frequented site. Tourists would be nearby in the future. Tibra had told her that. She knew people would not find her easily, even though she wanted to be found, but dogs could. Of course, tourists wouldn't bring dogs, soldiers might. And in any case, there weren't any tourists in North Africa at that moment, because of the fuel crisis. Tibra couldn't have known that, because she'd been in captivity too long. She tried to think clearly. The truth was, she didn't know what she knew. The walls were drawing closer together. Hot tears burned down her cheeks. The sound of scraping woke her. She rubbed her eyes. With the aid of a shovel, Tibra had removed a large square portion of the floor. Hilary passed down the lantern and waited. She was rewarded with an assortment of military supplies. The bobbing lantern made some items difficult to identify. However, no sooner had Tibra passed full water bottles to the surface, than Hilary was upon them.

CHAPTER 39

Simon Hawthorne joined Joshua Simmons in the almost deserted restaurant at the Holiday Inn a few hundred meters away from Andall Road Police station.

'I've nearly finished that list you asked me for, Inspector,' Simmons said. The oil expert looked worried even when he was eating. Hawthorne smiled. It wasn't until he bit into his cannelloni and tasted its shrivelled filling that the inspector realised he was eating tinned food.

'I've been eating this stuff all week. The hotel can't transport fresh supplies. I've gotten used to it!' the American academic exclaimed.

'What is it that you actually do for Brydale's company, Defence Consultants Limited?' the detective asked.

'My academic post is joint-funded by the oil industry and the US government,' the scholar remarked. 'And to put it in a nutshell, they both want the world's oil resources exploited more effectively and more efficiently. So they send people like me to study the way the industry works and suggest ways it could be done better.'

'Do you mean you actually tell Brydale how to guard an oilfield?' Hawthorne asked, putting down his knife and fork in surprise.

'Well, yes and no,' Simmons mused. 'We don't put army boots and helmets on, and wander around in the undergrowth, no. However, we do form close partnerships with private military agencies. The Pentagon's U.S. European Command has a role protecting US oil. Its action plan, Caspian Guard, focuses on Kazakhstan's Caspian Sea Region. The military command and the Colombian government have Plan Colombia, instead. I'm a consultant on both and Defence Consultants Limited is a partner in both strategies. That's the reason why I'm here.'

'But, wasn't Plan Colombia the United States' war on drugs?' Hawthorne remarked.

'It originally was,' Simmons agreed. 'But with a new administration our priorities have changed and it's now equally as concerned with guarding our country's oil supplies.'

The academic had only just finished speaking when a waiter hurried over towards their table, 'there's a telephone call for you in the hotel manager's officer, sir,' he said to Simmons. 'It's very urgent.' Simmons looked at the waiter and then he looked at Hawthorne.

'For me?' he said.

'Yes,' the waiter replied. 'The office is this way, sir.'

As Hawthorne watched Simmons being led away he scanned the empty restaurant. Close by, in an open lounge area, a television set was broadcasting a news report. Hawthorne moved closer to the screen.

'We've breaking news for you,' a well-groomed news anchorman declared. 'The American government has just announced that it believes Libya was behind the assassination of its most senior trade representative, Ambassador Whittler, last Thursday in Tripoli. We go now to our reporter outside the basement where Ambassador Whittler was killed. John, what more can you tell us?'

'That's right, Steven,' a casually dressed reporter agreed. The journalist was pictured standing in a narrow and dusty alleyway. 'This is the actual street in which Ambassador Whittler died,' he explained. 'The White House Trade Representative was carried up this street behind me now and loaded into an ambulance. You can't see where that happened because these streets are too narrow and too winding for that. There have been repeated reports since the death of Mr Whittler that he was personally carrying out a claim against the Libyan government for lost US revenues during the Eighties. The implication which has been made is that Mr Whittler died as a result of that dispute. The Libyan government have strenuously denied any involvement in the killing.'

Simmons returned looking shaken.

'Have you heard the news?' he asked.

'I have,' Hawthorne admitted. 'There are claims and counterclaims as there always are at times like these. But don't worry. None of this affects you.'

'But it does. Of course it does!' Doctor Simmons protested. 'It was my idea that Ambassador Whittler should go to Libya in the first place.'

'Oh,' Hawthorne said. 'What made you suggest that?'

'It wasn't a difficult decision, paradoxically. We had to go there. I don't know if you know that in the Nineteen Eighties Ronald

Reagan's administration forced all US companies to leave Libya. For well over a decade we left the oil drilling sites unmanned. It wasn't until the Libyan government threatened to sell our oilfields to our European rivals that the problems really started. My project, as you know, specialises in finding ways to protect US oil supplies and speed up the delivery of oil. The prospect of having functioning sites confiscated from us presented a setback, obviously. We needed to prevent that from happening and at the same time there are intense political feelings of animosity towards Libya at the highest levels of the US government. A high level solution was needed to settle the problem quickly and I came up with it. I told the ambassador to fly to Libya and ask Colonel Quadaffi not to sell our oilfields. In return we would gradually ease sanctions against his country and reopen diplomatic relations. It was a great gain for Libya at no real cost to us. The truth is, I don't believe they would have sold the oilfields, anyway. Not unless America snubbed Libya in public. They'd have done it then, just to spite us. Mine was the obvious solution.'

CHAPTER 40

'I've arrested Luke Connors,' Superintendent Jarvis announced to Hawthorne as the inspector returned from his lunch at the hotel.

'Oh, my god, why?' the detective exclaimed.

'Because this whole thing is turning into a full-scale international incident with us right in the middle of it! That's why. Because you're not doing your job properly. I'm having to do it for you. That's why. Come in here, man. Come in here,' Jarvis said, shuffling his bulky frame through his office door.

Hawthorne stood still while his superintendent shuffled papers on his desk.

'I want you to do something for me,' the fat man said. 'I want you to get the location of Hilary Connors out of the Connors boy.'

'He doesn't know where she is,' Hawthorne protested. 'None of us know where she is. That's what I've been trying to tell you.'

'I've heard all that,' Jarvis said, waiving a chubby hand through the air. 'But the major knows, doesn't he? And the boy knows where the major is. And get the information out of the solicitor about what Keith was up to before he died, will you, or do I have to do everything myself?'

Hawthorne stared at him.

'Well that's it, Inspector,' commanded Jarvis. 'Off you go.'

'We've arrested Luke Connors,' Sergeant Dalgliesh said to Hawthorne as the detective returned to his office.

'I know,' the inspector replied. 'I've just seen Jarvis.'

'Well,' Dalgliesh continued. 'What do you want me to do with him?'

The two men escorted Luke into the same interview room which had held them and Vincent Hanner a few hours earlier. Instinctively the sergeant moved to switch on the interview tape. Hawthorne reached out to stop him.

'Leave it off,' he said. The sergeant formed a protest with his mouth, but he remained silent.

'What am I doing here?' Luke asked.

'We need your help,' Hawthorne explained. 'You can leave this room now, if you want. You're free to go. But we need your help.'

'How?' Luke asked. 'I've already told you everything I know. I even gave the major to you and look where that got us. I can't do any more. Can I?'

'There's your solicitor, Cardman,' the detective suggested. 'You could help us with him.'

'Tell me what you want, and if I can do it, I'll do it,' the student replied. Hawthorne opened his mouth and then closed it again.

'Go straight home,' he said opening the interview room door. 'I've got to think about this.'

Luke rose and hesitated, then he left the room.

'What is it, sir?' Dalgliesh asked. 'What's the matter?'

'There's something not right about Cardman. I can't tell you what it is. We know that he had intimate knowledge of all Keith's business affairs. We know Keith and Cardman even discussed individual plans. What if we send that boy in there to ask detailed questions about his father's affairs and the same thing which happened to his father happens to him? What then?'

'Do you think there's a risk of that?' the sergeant asked.

'Yes,' said Hawthorne. 'Yes I do.'

'Well then, it's simple,' Dalgliesh said. 'We don't do it.'

'We'll see,' the inspector said, climbing to his feet. 'I don't think it's that simple at all.'

Superintendent Jarvis was red-faced.

'You've let him go!' he shouted. 'You've let him go! I've made the first break in this case. I've arrested the Connors boy. I gave you one simple thing to do and you couldn't get that right. I tell you, Inspector, I've had just about enough of this!'

Hawthorne said nothing. Uniformed officers had begun to collect in the hallway outside his office.

'Well,' Jarvis challenged. 'What have you got to say for yourself?'

'What was I supposed to charge him with?' Hawthorne asked. 'I can't very well go around charging people with having a mother who's out of the country. Can I? That's not a crime. Well at least not yet, it's not.'

'I didn't tell you to charge him with anything, did I?' Jarvis yelled. 'I said find out where the Connors woman is. That's not charging him, is it? I asked one reasonable thing. Why couldn't you do that?'

'He doesn't know where she is. That's what I've been saying. He doesn't know,' Hawthorne insisted.

'How do you know what he knows, if you don't ask him?' the superintendent responded. 'Sergeant, re-arrest him.'

'No, don't do that, Sergeant. Stay here,' Hawthorne countered. The sergeant watched the two men argue momentarily and then stepped outside the office, closing the door.

'What the hell are you all looking at?' Dalgliesh demanded of the staff in the hall. The assembled group dispersed.

'I've a good mind to suspend you!' Jarvis yelled.

'I can understand that, sir,' the inspector replied. 'Are you going to suspend me or do you want me to solve this case?'

'Can you solve it?' the superintendent asked.

'I think so,' Hawthorne told him. 'You're right about one thing. The solicitor is definitely the key, but it's obviously his duty to protect his dead client's privileges, so he won't tell us what he knows. If he told Luke then the boy would be in danger too, obviously.'

'So what do you suggest?' Jarvis grunted.

'I suggest we frighten the solicitor, sir,' Hawthorne explained. 'I suggest we scare the living daylights out of him and then wait for him to come to us.'

CHAPTER 41

Hilary would have quenched her thirst, immediately, had it not been for the fact that the simple act of drawing the canister to her lips conjured up images of her stricken friend. While she deliberated, the loose cap tapped against the aluminium flank of her water-bottle. The light below the floor flickered as Tibra pushed it back into the passage above her. With her throat still dry, Hilary re-fastened the bottle-cap and returned the flask to the pile.

With the others, she and Tibra shared dried dates and two mouthfuls of water each. Aemelia had more. They settled down, with the blankets spread equally unevenly between them. Hilary woke beside her friend. She stroked the young woman's hair while she watched Tibra silently packing their few possessions. Then she gathered the others, and together, for the first time, they climbed into the Unimog's cabin. They twisted upwards towards the cliff-face, slowly. Taking with her several empty flasks, their driver paused to reconnoitre. The others waited, using their time to replenish the fuel tank from the petrol rack. Eventually, Tibra returned and their truck emerged from the cavern into the half-light, on the side of a chalky-pale, looming, jagged mountain. Tibra weaved over a rough, zig-zagging track and descended, to reach a flat, limitless, barren wasteland, where here and there a rocky outcrop or an itinerant group of camels broke up the otherwise endless nothingness. And then, for hours, by the light of the full moon, they drove. Early the next morning, in the midst of the arid plain, they squeezed against a group of rocks, where, for most of the day, they slept or fidgeted, while hiding from the repressive heat. Later, in twilight, they journeyed until Tibra steered under an arch into an ancient Berber village, drawing them deep inside a covered passage.

'No people,' she observed, pointing in all directions, while leading them from the passage into an adobe dwelling which joined onto it at one end. With the exception of Aemelia, all the women drew water from the well, under the low, recently whitewashed, covered archway at the end of the adjacent, open passage. Tibra left them, and returned hours later leading a mule. Hilary watched incredulously as she distributed fresh clothing and supplies among the group.

'Where does all this come from?' she asked.

Tibra smiled. 'Ghadames, new,' she rippled her hands and shoulders enigmatically, 'Ghadames, old.'

Hilary nodded. It was an explanation, she supposed, but she didn't believe four fugitives could simply turn up anywhere and be resupplied completely free of charge, not even in this god-forsaken place, wherever it might be. She felt sure, there had to be a cost associated with this bounty. She simply had no idea what it could possibly be. No matter, she wasn't about to refuse. She took the clothes, the soap and the food, and ducked back into the dwelling. Under the low sloping roof inside the courtyard, she scrubbed her whole body fiercely, uttering curious moaning sounds as she did so, to which she alone was oblivious.

When they awoke, Tibra was nowhere to be seen. Hilary stepped into the cool, covered passage, itself sheltered from the fierce sunlight which baked the floor and mud-lined walls of the narrow close beyond. Climbing the dried and dusty steps which cut into the wall at the base of the courtyard, beneath several overhanging palms, she marvelled at the tall, mud and lime buildings and the minarets which dwarfed even the tallest trees in the centre of the old town. From close by, somewhere in the street below, the sound of voices rose and she retreated hastily. As evening fell, the group reformed and Tibra drove them into the desert once more. In silence, they jutted across miles of stony plains.

Slowing, to point out two tall, thin piles of rocks, about the height of a person, their driver commented, 'Algerie border.'

Hilary couldn't see anything special. Beyond the stones there was an endless expanse of desert and other than that, there wasn't anything at all. Tibra looked at her impassive passengers briefly and accelerated. Picking her way through the undulating ocean of sand which now surrounded them, Tibra flashed her headlights a number of times in quick succession. In the gloom, it was some time before Hilary realised that a number of shapes in front of them were approaching. At first, the shapes were indistinct, and then they could clearly be identified as riders. Several more appeared above the slope behind. Hilary shook the others. In two rows, blocking the track in front of the lorry, the tribesmen stopped. Tibra walked forward and as she did so, the lead camel sank to the ground. Its rider lurched forward and then backwards as the great beast tucked its hind legs onto the desert floor.

CHAPTER 42

They watched Tibra's outline move among the riders. Those others, still some distance behind them, stood out clearly, silhouetted on the ridges above them. Without hurrying, their driver returned. She moved the Unimog forward slowly, sandwiched between the two clusters of desert tribesmen. In this formation, they threaded themselves along the valley floor, which snaked between the stretched-out, serrated cliffs of sand. Some way off, Hilary could make out a series of white spots against the blackness. Eventually, their awkward caravan stopped at a campfire in the centre of the valley. An old nomad, whose soft, brown eyes smiled through the single gap in his deep blue turban, placed wood sparingly into the flickering fire, as someone might, who was used to conserving scarce resources in the barren and unforgiving desert.

The Tuareg dismounted, leading their camels some distance away. There, each mount was constrained with a pair of goatskin ankle-tethers. The old man gave each fugitive a maroon and grey-striped, tightly woven, woollen mat. Close to the fire he wrapped Hilary and the child together. He and Tibra examined Aemelia's wrists in the firelight. They wrapped her more carefully than the others, and crouched together, talking for some time.

As the old man spoke, the others watched Tibra dig a low, shallow hole, into which she transferred some of the burning twigs. With charcoal, brought forward by the old man, their able guide built a makeshift oven. She stretched and twisted a dough-ball which she turned above the flames for a period, before burying it in the hot sand. By the time her desert-bread had cooked, Tibra had divided an aromatic onion and tomato sauce into two bowls before her on the ground. They settled around the fire to eat in two small groups. Then, in the cool sand, where her followers were about to lie down for the night, Tibra scattered and re-buried the still smouldering charcoals. All night, wrapped twice in their mats, together with every blanket they possessed, the escapees lay huddled beside the fire, with their bodies touching and the child pressed between them. The old nomad, whose blue-swaddled face had become still further hidden behind the campfire's darting, amber tongues, chattered softly to himself as he contemplated the addition of each stick.

Tibra nudged Hilary awake in the chilly dawn air. Reluctantly, as the heavens unfurled a carpet of light across the desert, she crawled from her covers. The old man, who'd been asleep sitting-up, twisted to watch her clambering up the shifting inside of the sandy embankment in Tibra's wake. She had almost decided on a list of questions but now was concentrating instead on her frosted clouds of breath. Her distraction had not helped her to organise the questions in her head. But she still had a couple of seconds left before she caught up with her friend. She dug into the soft sand harder, in order to make up the remaining distance between them.

And then at the summit, she saw what Tibra had woken her for: Above the horizon, a rioting, bright and swirling canopy of crimson, yellow, golden and violet, perforated with great gashes of pale blue advanced steadily towards them, pushing the edges of the dull night sky before it like the ragged, chaotic lines of a routed army. She didn't ask any questions. Instead, transfixed, she stood staring upwards at the breathtaking desert-sunrise. Her companion smiled, clasped her shoulder and then turned and trotted back to the camp to tend to the dying fire.

That day, for the first time, they moved in broad daylight. The women grouped together in the lorry's cabin, Tibra among them. Her place behind the wheel taken over now by the old man, covered from head to foot in his blue robes, and gripping the wheel with his leathery hands, as though battling some great vessel, caught-up in a gale at sea. The Unimog had no difficulty with tackling the small ridges. But when they started to get bigger, their driver was forced to make ever larger detours in order to find a way through.

Hilary's breathing had become strained. Now they were sucking in bone-dry air, which burned into their lungs. Sometimes they swallowed the dust, when they couldn't spit it out. A film of fine sand was everywhere and covered everything, clothes, hair, eyes and food. Ahead of them, every so often, lay pockets of powder. Each one they hit caused the Unimog to disappear in a dense, yellow plume. With the exception of Aemilia, all the fugitives were kept busy, wiping the windscreen, so their guide could see where he was going. By now Hilary could make out a black and green rock formation someway off in the distance. As they approached, not always directly, the tiny mountain took shape. Its darkened cliff-face, like the keep of a charred and ruined medieval castle, stripped of its outer defences, protruded from the dunes, piled together against its base. The track which they were following skirted the outermost ridge and dipped behind a natural, rocky buttress. The old man brought the exhausted, gasping group to rest in the shade beneath an overhanging rock-face.

CHAPTER 43

'You can come back in now, Sergeant,' Hawthorne called out. 'There's something we all agree on and that is that Cardman, Luke and Keith's solicitor, is the key to all of this. He's the closest thing Keith ever had to a confidant. He knows exactly what went on before Keith died. He knows what Ambassador Whittler had so urgently to speak to Connors about. The Americans don't know about Cardman, yet. But it won't take them long to track him down and then we'll lose him.'

'We'll have to bring him in then, sir,' Dalgliesh concluded. 'The problem is: What can we pick him up for? And how can we make him talk? He's a solicitor and at the risk of stating the obvious, he knows that he doesn't have to say anything if he doesn't want to. If we pick him up we'll only have to release him again in a few hours time. And what will that have gained us?'

'We'll have to think of something,' Superintendent Jarvis chided. 'We can't bring him in and we can't leave him out. What can we do?'

'The group does have an Achilles heel, sir,' Hawthorne remarked. 'The most vulnerable person in Keith's circle is Bob, his photography partner. Bob took naked photographs of Nancy. We still don't know what Major Carter meant when he said Hilary thought Bob was involved in Keith's death. It might have been a crude attempt to deflect attention away from Hilary. If we can compromise Bob enough we might find something to put pressure on the solicitor with.'

'Didn't I hear you say something about naked photographs of a young girl?' Jarvis interrupted.

'Nancy's daughter Monique. Yes, sir, you did. But they weren't taken by Bob. They were taken by Keith and Nancy. They sold them too. Hang on,' Hawthorne said. 'That's it!'

'Hang on what?' Jarvis replied. 'What's what?'

'The photographs,' Hawthorne explained. 'How did Keith know who to sell the photographs to? He's an engineer. How would an engineer know how to find a market in underaged, salacious photographs? And Nancy, who has been a prostitute and still sells sex services from her computer at home, said that she got Keith to help her to sell the photos, and not the other way around, which is what you might expect. I've got to pay Nancy another visit. Sergeant, can you get a warrant to search Bob's studio and his house?'

'On what grounds, sir?' Dalgliesh asked.

'He and Keith were business partners. But Keith had a weapon to threaten Bob with: Nancy's photographs,' Hawthorne replied.

Nancy opened her patio door and looked past the detective into the street.

'Where are the others?' she said.

'There aren't any,' he told her. 'I'm on my own.'

It was the first time, apart from when she had dressed earlier to accompany him to the police station that the detective had seen Mrs Collimore with all her clothes on. She looked surprisingly ordinary.

'What's the matter?' Nancy asked, pausing in the centre of her kitchen.

'Nothing,' Hawthorne said quickly. 'I need to ask you about the photographs of Monique again.'

'What about them?' said Nancy. There was a sharp edge to her voice now.

'You said Keith sold them. Who did he sell them to?'

'She was sixteen,' Nancy pleaded. 'They were legal. It wasn't a moral thing to have done, but it wasn't illegal.'

'I'm not interested in the rights and wrongs of it, Nancy,' Hawthorne explained. 'I need help. Please just tell me. Who did Keith sell the photographs to?'

'He sold them to lots of people,' Nancy explained. 'I told you, didn't I, that I've known Keith for more than twenty years, haven't I? I knew Keith when he didn't have his fancy house and lots of expensive cars. He had wealthy parents though. Keith always had everything he wanted. That's why he always thought he could use people, just use them up and get rid of them when they'd served his purposes. He's a bastard. Have you seen his wife's scar?' The edge had returned into Nancy's voice.

'Sorry, Nancy,' Hawthorne prompted. 'Can we get back to who bought the photographs?'

'The photographs?' she said.

'The photographs of Monique. Keith sold the photographs of Monique. Who did he sell them to?'

'Oh, he sold those to Brian Cardman,' she said. 'Well, I don't know if he sold them or gave them to him to sell. He said he'd get my husband's money back and he did. He knew Brian wanted the pictures anyway. Keith and Brian went to school together. And they both went to university with that irritating man with the French surname. The one who works with Brian.'

'Did Keith actually tell you what he did with the photographs?' the detective asked.

'Of course he did. I knew anyway. It's no secret that Brian and his friends collect pictures of naked girls. The difference between them and Keith was that as Keith got older, so did the girls in his pictures. That wasn't the case with Brian. Keith left home and got married, and Brian didn't.'

'Can I get you to write all that down?' Hawthorne asked her.

Nancy nodded.

'If you want me to,' she said. 'Do you want a drink?'

'No thanks,' the detective said. 'I'm just going to take your statement and rush back to the station.'

'Can I ask you a personal question?' she said.

'OK,' Hawthorne replied. 'Do I have to answer it?'

'What did you think of my photographs?'

The detective twisted his neck fully round and stared at her.

'What did I think?' he said. 'Oh, God! I don't know what I thought. I suppose my first thought was does Mick know about these? Given that Keith had them, I suppose my first thought was does Mick know about you and Keith?'

'That wasn't what I meant,' Nancy explained. She brought a glass of vermouth for herself and another for him, placing his glass beside him on the floor. Then she undid the top two buttons of her blouse.

'What I meant was: What did you think of the photographs? They're well done, aren't they?'

CHAPTER 44

At first the detective didn't react. He couldn't agree and nor could he disagree.

'Can we write your statement down,' he pleaded. 'Let's talk about your photographs another time.'

'Don't you like them?' Nancy asked. 'What do you want me to write?'

Hawthorne watched as she formed smooth words in round, girlish handwriting. He put his hands together on her kitchen work-surface and began to relax. Even though he was reading upside down, the detective could tell that she'd reached the part about Keith's schooldays. He looked at his watch. While he was distracted, Nancy placed her left hand on top of his. Hawthorne pulled his arms backwards quickly. His hostess stopped writing. In her statement the part about Monique's photographs was missing. They both knew that without it his investigation could not proceed.

'You want something from me and I want something from you,' Nancy said, caressing her lips with the top of her pen and then licking its tip. 'What's it going to be?'

He was transfixed.

'I can't believe you're doing this,' he protested. 'Can't you just finish and sign the statement?'

She crossed the room, retrieving their drinks and kissed his cheek as she returned to her seat.

'I was only teasing you,' Nancy explained. 'What did you think I was doing? You men always take everything so seriously.'

As his hostess began writing again, Simon Hawthorne let out a sigh. He hadn't noticed before, but his heart was pounding in his chest.

'If I give you this, will you buy me dinner?' Nancy asked, holding her statement towards the detective.

'You can ask me,' Hawthorne replied taking the statement. 'When this case is over you can walk right into the police station and ask me. We don't want any rumours about favours before that, do we?'

She took his coat towards her patio door, only giving it to him when he was outside on the step. Then Nancy kissed him again.

'Don't forget, dinner,' she reminded him.

'I won't forget,' Hawthorne replied. 'Believe me, I won't forget.' And then he ran. There was at least half a mile between Nancy's house and Andall Road Police Station. Hawthorne ran all the way without stopping.

'Where's the engineer?' he gasped as Dalgliesh met him outside the police canteen.

'Are you alright, sir?' his sergeant asked.

'The en…, the engine…, the engineer,' Hawthorne panted. 'Get the phone engineer.'

Despite the lateness of the hour, the cycle shop on Andall High Street was still doing a brisk trade. Everything else was shuttered. The high street's only remaining newsagent advertised the long awaited end of the fuel crisis, in giant, red lettering, on the inside of its dimly lit window. Stebson, the engineer, paused, lowered his toolkit and flexed his arms. Hawthorne grabbed the case and hurried him on. Most of the office lights were out in Commercial Dock Business Park, except for those on the floor of the building which Luke Connors' solicitor shared with his accountant. Hawthorne pushed the door lightly and stepped inside. Two floors up, the lift stopped in front of the receptionist's vacant desk. From beyond, raised voices could be heard.

The first said clearly, '…realise, we have to tell them?'

Something heavy landed on the floor, with a thud.

Another voice, lower this time, replied, 'you won't tell them anything! I'll make damn sure of that. That's always been your problem, Christopher; you've got no backbone!'

Dalgliesh and Hawthorne strode quickly to Cardman's office door. The shouting ceased. The detectives stopped. And then, as Dalgliesh reached for Cardman's door handle, the office door opened. In a bright light, framed against the dark-wood doorway, Delatouche stood clasping and unclasping his hands. Behind him was Luke's solicitor. The three plain-clothed policemen watched Cardman pick a marble bust up off his office floor. He stood in the centre of his room, with his chest heaving, unconsciously running his fingers over the smooth surface of the figure.

'I don't want you discussing any of this with anyone, Christopher! Do I make myself clear?' Cardman shouted after the retreating accountant. Delatouche made no reply. Instead, he walked quickly towards the open lift. The inspector stepped into Cardman's room and closed the door.

'I hope you don't mind if I come in?' he asked, seating himself in the solicitor's visitors' chair.

'Suit yourself. I can only spare you a minute at the most. I was on my way home just as you arrived,' Cardman told him.

'Yes, we noticed that,' Hawthorne acknowledged, twisting the marble figurehead on the solicitor's desk towards him.

'I thought you might like to know, we know about your photograph collection. Did you buy any of it from Keith Connors?' Hawthorne asked. Then he added, 'we're searching your house.' Cardman swallowed hard.

'I don't know what you're talking about,' he said faintly. 'What are you searching my house for? What photographs?' Hawthorne climbed to his feet.

'I'm going to have to take you with me to the station, I'm afraid. We're searching this office now too. I'll ask some constables to join you,' Hawthorne promised Dalgliesh. 'Take up the floorboards and the drains, if you have to.'

When the detective and the solicitor stepped outside, the air was crisp. The instant that he left Cardman's office, Hawthorne sensed the feeling that now he knew so well. He was being watched. The detective pulled his collar around his neck and steered Cardman towards the car park entrance. They crossed the road from the undeveloped side of Andall Station's main railway line. Hawthorne turned. He couldn't see anybody, but behind him somewhere, he could hear the sound of several sets of footsteps gaining on them.

CHAPTER 45

As they neared the level-crossing opposite the north-west entrance to Commercial Dock Business Park, Hawthorne began to hurry Cardman along. A few yards ahead of him Andall's railway split with a line crossing an iron bridge to the city-side of the dock's disused canal. Here the road and railway bridge were separated by a low, tapering, concrete platform, which was overgrown and litter-strewn. The open space between the well-lit park entrance and the first functioning street light on the city-side of the canal was pitch dark. Inside the right pocket of his navy overcoat, the detective gripped his keys, so that they protruded from his clenched fist. He knew that his keys didn't make much of a weapon, but they were all he had. The footsteps ceased, and from somewhere on the far side of the railway bridge he heard muffled voices. He looked behind. It was as far now to a source of light in either direction. Two dark figures spanned the gap ahead of them, between the bridge and the road. A third followed. Behind, a fourth figure emerged. When Cardman and Hawthorne crossed the road, the two sets of figures were equidistant. The detective retraced his steps towards the lone stranger. As he turned, the trio ahead broke into a run. He swivelled, seconds before they met. The lead assailant, separated from his companions by several metres, flailed his arms to counteract his own forward momentum. But it was too late. Hawthorne struck at the man's exposed neck. The force gathered from the inspector's turning blow sent his opponent sprawling face up into some trackside weeds, clutching his throat. Vaulting his felled comrade's jittering legs, the next attacker landed squarely in front of the detective. Hawthorne stepped backwards and his assailant drove the crown of his head into the inspector's face. Others joined in. As blows from all sides rained down, Hawthorne covered his head and sank to the ground. And then suddenly, it all stopped.

Two lights shone in his face. The wounded detective lashed out at a hand which had taken hold of his left shoulder. A capped figure, partially illuminated by one of the lights, asked him something about being alright. The same figure threw a bicycle against the concrete platform. Hawthorne leaned forward to stem the bleeding from his nose.

'Are you alright, sir?' the bicycle owner asked again, pointing a high-powered torch into Hawthorne's battered face. Hawthorne coughed, spitting a mixture of blood and phlegm onto the ground between his legs, as he turned to watch another constable crossing the wasteland behind them. During that second Hawthorne suddenly remembered he hadn't travelled on his own.

'Where's Cardman?' he asked his assistant.

'Where's who, sir?' the younger man responded.

'I came here with another person? Where is he?' Hawthorne said, twisting his torso this way and that. He rose and lost his balance, swerving into the constable's bicycle. Its owner took the inspector under the arm and led him to the foot of the railway bridge. There on the ground a twisted figure lay face upwards. Hawthorne started to run.

'He's breathing,' the constable volunteered.

'Can you point that thing down?' Hawthorne replied sweeping the constable's torch away from his own face.

'Hold on a second,' Hawthorne said. 'That's not Cardman. That's Vincent Hanner. He's already on bail for assaulting Luke Connors.'

'Do you want us to arrest him, sir?' The constable approaching from the wasteland asked, removing his handcuffs from his belt.

'Hardly, Constable,' Hawthorne snapped, spitting onto the ground between them. 'He's not going anywhere, is he? Find Cardman!' The inspector spat more blood, wiped his mouth with his wrist and stepped forward shouting Cardman's name.

Dalgliesh emerged from Cardman's office block. He was speaking into his radio and listening to a uniformed constable both at the same time.

'What happened, sir?' the sergeant asked. 'You need to see a doctor.'

'Get ten men and get to Delatouche's house as quick as you can,' Hawthorne hissed. 'Hurry, for God's sake.'

CHAPTER 46

In a curtained-off cubicle, tucked inside the subterranean entrance of Andall Road General Hospital's accident and emergency ward, Simon Hawthorne waited for a doctor to complete an examination of Vincent Hanner's neck injuries. The detective, who was pulling towels from the wall-mounted dispenser, caught a glimpse of his own face in a mirror and exclaimed, 'oh, Christ!'

The doctor looked up.

'Has anybody taken a look at that wound, Inspector?' he enquired.

The detective ran the index finger of his right hand over the bridge of his nose. Then he washed the blood from his hand as he dampened another paper towel.

'I think it looks worse than it really is,' he replied, in a distorted, nasal voice. Hawthorne crossed the cubicle, while still wiping his face and motioned towards the patient. The man on the bed, who now had both eyes open, was trying to raise himself. He looked at Hawthorne for a few seconds. Then he looked at the doctor and back towards Hawthorne.

'What,' Hanner said, clearing his throat. 'What am I doing here?' Then he shook his wrists, both of which were handcuffed to his bed and added, 'and what the fuck is this?'

'Vincent Hanner, I'm arresting you for assaulting a police officer, abduction and false imprisonment,' Hawthorne told him. 'Now, where's Brian Cardman?'

Hanner laughed.

'I'm lying here chained to a hospital bed and you're asking me where Brian Cardman is! What the fuck's wrong with you?'

Hawthorne pressed his face almost against Vincent's and shouted back.

'I've got a broken fucking nose! That's what the fuck's wrong with me and you broke it. Now where the fuck is Cardman?'

'You did this!' Hanner screamed, shaking his neck brace. 'You did! I'm going to fucking sue the living fuck out of you! I didn't break your fucking nose it was Da...'

The detective smiled and pulled back the cubicle curtain to reveal a small crowd of uniformed officers.

'Two of you inside,' he told them. 'Two of you outside. If he wants to go to the bathroom I want you to go with him. Don't let him out of your sight. Not even for a second. The rest of you, come with me.'

At the entrance to the hospital ward Superintendent Jarvis met them. He had sweat pouring from his face.

'What, what the hell happened, man?' he panted. 'And what's happened to your face?'

'We were attacked outside Brian Cardman's office by Vincent Hanner, one of his known associates Darryl Pitt, and a third person who we haven't yet identified, sir,' Hawthorne explained. 'Cardman disappeared during the attack.'

'You'd better explain,' Superintendent Jarvis instructed. 'People could get hurt, for God's sake! People have already been hurt. What the hell is going on?'

'I think my plan worked,' Hawthorne replied. 'I wanted to frighten Cardman and I succeeded. I just didn't realise that he'd react in such a spectacular fashion. I had no way of knowing he'd actually attack me.'

'How do you know Cardman attacked you?' Jarvis insisted. 'I thought you said it was Hanner.'

'Hanner doesn't do anything without instructions. He simply does what he's told. That's why he confessed to assaulting Luke. Brydale told him to confess so that we'd have nothing to investigate. It'll be exactly the same in this case. The difference though is that this time we're not investigating an assault, sir. We're investigating a murder.'

'Hold on, hold on,' Jarvis instructed. 'Where are we going anyway? Are you trying to tell me Brydale and Cardman killed Connors? What the hell for, for God's sake? They both benefited most from his being alive. Brydale got security contracts and Cardman got whopping great solicitor's fees. I think you're barking up the wrong tree there, Inspector. Unless you've got evidence, of course.'

'I've sent Sergeant Dalgliesh to fetch Keith's accountant, Delatouche. He can explain it all. The only thing is, we've got to get to him before Cardman and Brydale do. They know he's already at breaking point. I heard them arguing about it.'

'We're getting pretty close to the Marchant Estates,' Jarvis warned. 'I want you to stop and explain. What exactly is going on? This looks dangerous to me.'

The night air was cold and the water vapour of the policemen's breaths hung in clouds about their faces. They were standing on the same patch of open waste ground which Hawthorne had assembled Operation Extract's mounted riot police on a few days earlier. This time there were only nine of them and none had shields or helmets. The uniformed officers had protective vests. But their peaked hats were made from felt and offered no protection. Hawthorne and Jarvis had no protection of any kind, not even a baton.

'I think we've been right about Keith Connors all the time. There's no secret about the fact that he advised the oil companies in Nigeria to lease helicopters to the Nigerian soldiers who were massacring the Ogoni villagers. He also advised the companies in Colombia to commission the murders of trades unionists and their villagers too. We suspected it, sir, and we were right. I still don't have the final proof. But I will have it when we get Delatouche. First we have to stop Cardman and Brydale and to do that we need to enter the Marchant Housing Estate.'

Somewhere in the centre of the housing complex before them a dog barked. Hawthorne moved closer.

'Wait! We need reinforcements,' Jarvis insisted.

'There's no time,' Hawthorne replied. 'By the time you've got the whole of Operation Extract kitted up and brought all the way out here our evidence will have been destroyed and Delatouche will be dead. They think they're out of reach of the law here. We have to go now, sir, just the way we are.'

CHAPTER 47

'Alright,' Jarvis hissed. 'I'll stay here and get as many men to join me as I can. You go on.'

'Who'll come with me?' Hawthorne asked. All seven uniformed men volunteered.

By now Hawthorne was familiar with the southernmost entrance to the Marchant Housing Estate. The moonlit drug dealing dens beneath Mandela House looked eerily deserted. The men filed past in silence. Seconds later they heard voices. Three singing adults, all holding bottles and approaching from Victoria House ahead, stopped beside an abandoned car and one began to urinate. Following the inspector's example the officers flattened themselves against a nearby wall. When the revellers had gone, at a rapid pace, the group traversed the space between the two groups of flats and ascended the stairwell in Victoria House. Hawthorne led them to the flat which had once held Vincent Hanner. Without pausing he launched himself at its front door. As the splintering wood gave way, Hawthorne's men rushed in. Two ran upstairs and one into the kitchen. A woman screamed. Brydale, who was sitting at the dining room table and had what looked like a blood-soaked dishcloth wrapped around his right hand, swore and jumped to his feet. Cardman did nothing. He was sitting on a leather sofa opposite the table when the officers burst in. Hawthorne took two steps towards the wounded man. He retreated and opening a glass door behind him with his good hand, stepped outside onto a balcony. Two officers removed a telephone from Cardman and handcuffed him. Hawthorne followed Brydale into the darkness. On the outside of each flat a brace of tapered walls led down into the balcony of the flat below. The old soldier vaulted onto one of them and scrambled out of reach. Seconds later Hawthorne watched him jump from the lowest garden of all onto the courtyard at the foot of the building and run into the middle of the estate.

'Do you want us to go after him, sir?' one of Hawthorne's men asked.

'Let him go,' Hawthorne said. 'I know where he's going.'

'What are you arresting me for?' Cardman asked.

'Brian Cardman, I'm arresting you on suspicion of having committed offences contravening Section One, Paragraph One A of the Protection of Children Act, Nineteen Seventy Eight,' the detective said. 'You do not have to say anything. But it may harm your defence if you do not mention when questioned something which you later rely on in court. Anything you do say may be given in evidence.'

'I hope you know what you're doing, Inspector,' Cardman replied. 'Because if you don't, when I've finished with you, Section One of the Protection of Children Act will be the least of your worries, believe me!'

'What do you want to do now, sir?' a constable standing at the front door asked. 'We're attracting attention. It's nothing heavy at the moment. But they know we're here.'

'Is there any sight of Jarvis?' the inspector asked.

'No, sir,' came the reply. 'I mean I don't know. I haven't looked.'

Hawthorne shot the constable a withering glance and stormed outside into the alley which ran between the flats. There were two youths outside, one of whom he knew.

'I hate fucking coons!' the boy shouted, retrieving his mobile phone and taking pictures of Hawthorne with it. Within minutes the boys had drawn a small crowd. Lights began to come on in windows all along the aisle and it wasn't long before balconies began to fill up with observers. Hawthorne telephoned Dalgliesh.

'Where are you?' he said.

'I'm at Delatouche's house,' the sergeant said. 'He's here. What do you want me to do with him?'

'Listen carefully,' Hawthorne told him. 'I want you to do several things and I want them all done quickly. We're going to be in a spot of bother here in a minute. We're in Vincent Hanner's flat on the Marchant. There are only eight of us and we're stuck. Things are starting to develop the way they always do. So we need help. That's the first thing. The second thing is that I want you to get Delatouche inside the police station and under lock and key as fast as you can. And the third thing is that I want you to dispatch part of Operation Extract to arrest Brydale at his base on Andall Airport. He might be armed. He knows we're coming. Have you got all that?'

'I've got it,' Dalgliesh replied. 'We'll get to you as soon as we can.'

The inspector called one of the constables over to him. 'Get water and mats and put them inside the door,' he said. 'If we get stuck inside and someone sets fire to the front of the house I want us to be ready. Just thank God there isn't any petrol left on the estate.'

'They can still use alcohol, sir,' the officer cautioned.

'They can but they won't, Constable. Hawthorne replied. 'When have you ever known anyone on this housing estate to throw away good alcohol?'

As he spoke a column of police officers in riot gear moved towards him down the alley. A few seconds later their leader had reached him and lifted the visor on his helmet.

'I gather that you're in a spot of bother,' the unit commander said. 'Do you want to follow us out?'

'How did you get here so quickly,' Hawthorne replied. 'We've only just got here ourselves.

'We've been here all day,' the unit commander explained. 'We've been arresting the ringleaders of Tuesday's riot.'

CHAPTER 48

'We've got Cardman in cell one, Vincent Hanner in the cell next to him and Delatouche in interview room one,' Sergeant Dalgliesh explained to a very tired inspector. 'Who do you want to see first? And by the way, Detective Chief Superintendent Trent radioed our operations room five minutes ago to say that Brydale isn't in his hut at the airport.'

'Has anyone tried pinging his mobile phone?' Hawthorne snapped. 'He's there somewhere.'

Hawthorne was shown the prisoners by Andall Road Police Station's custody sergeant. Cardman looked almost serene. He had taken his shoes off. He was sitting cross-legged on his thin, blue mattress and concentrating on the wall in front of him. Vincent Hanner, still in his neck brace, appeared more nervous. To Hawthorne the cause of the prisoner's worries looked more serious than two charges of assault. Further down the corridor in interview room one, Delatouche seemed to be beside himself. First he stood up and then he sat down. All the time he spent wringing his hands. Hawthorne sat and watched him.

'Would you like a drink?' he said at last.

'A drink?' the accountant replied. 'Yes, I mean no. I don't want a drink. In fact, I want to go to the lavatory.'

'Be my guest,' the detective said. 'It's through those doors and on the left.'

Delatouche sat down.

'What's going to happen to me?' he asked.

'It all depends,' Hawthorne explained. 'We'll prepare a file on you and hand it to the Crown Prosecution Service in just the same way as we will with all the others. Whether or not they will prosecute you with it will be a matter for them. I can't say what they'll do. I honestly don't know. But they'll listen to our recommendations. And in a pre-trial or a trial so will a judge or a magistrate.'

'It's all Brian's fault,' Delatouche wailed. 'I told him this would happen. I told him and I told him, but he wouldn't listen.'

Hawthorne smiled.

'Yes,' he said.

'I told him to own up about the pictures. He said he couldn't. He said it would ruin him. But I asked him which was worse, being ruined or being at the beck-and-call of a man like Keith Connors. I told him to own up about the pictures and be done with it.'

'Well, yes,' Hawthorne said.

'I knew what he was up to right from the beginning,' Delatouche asserted. 'He confided in Brian in the mid Nineties during the Saro-Wiwa scandal. Brian wouldn't represent him. He said they were too close. But he did give Keith advice and he confided in me, you see. So I knew exactly what was going on all the time.'

'Well, of course,' the inspector agreed. 'I can imagine.'

'They destroyed the two rural towns of Umuechem and Odi as well as more than thirty villages, leased helicopters to the soldiers who were massacring the civilians and even admitted that they had supplied guns to the Nigerian government.'

'Yes, I know. I remember,' the detective said.

'Did you know they were all Keith's ideas?' said Delatouche.

'I didn't know that. How do you know?' Hawthorne prompted.

'I was in Brian's office when Keith telephoned. He called after the massacres, which took place in Delta State. The media had obtained pictures of helicopters and boats, with Keith's company's logo on them, being used by soldiers to hunt down villagers and kill them. Keith was in a terrible state. Not because the people had been murdered. He hardly mentioned that at all. He was too big a bastard to worry about the suffering of other people. He was only anxious about his own safety. The thing which concerned Keith was that the aircraft and the speed boats were so obviously traceable to him. Brian advised him to say that the Nigerian military had commandeered the machines and that he had no choice but to hand them over. That's what he did say in the end. But he was still permanently linked to the massacres. The power of those iconic photographs of branded oil company vehicles being used to slaughter defenceless villages as they ran away, has never faded. And the companies have Keith to thank for that.'

'Well,' Hawthorne exclaimed, expelling air forcefully from his lungs and clasping his hands to his mouth. 'I'm surprised the two stayed friends after that.'

'Keith said that he had done with the oil companies. I knew the truth. The truth was that the oil companies had done with him.

People think the oil world is a big one. In some ways that's true, but everyone knows everyone else. You can be sure of that. In those days all you had to do was say 'Keith Connors' and anyone who heard you would reply 'wasn't he the one who supplied the boats for the Delta State massacres?' He was damaged goods, Inspector. Nobody would employ him, and to tell you the truth, I was glad. I'll tell you something else, Inspector. Even his own wife hated him. Did you know he once nearly killed her?'

'No, I didn't know that. What do you mean?' Hawthorne replied.

'Oh yes,' Delatouche insisted. He stood up. 'Oh yes. Didn't you know? Those statues in his garden, they are made of different stones. That wasn't always the case. In a fit of temper he pushed a statue over onto Hilary. She was crushed and still bears the scars today. She never forgave him for that. He deserved to die. The world is a better place without him.'

'Now that you've explained all this to me I can understand why Hilary had her husband killed. But what I don't understand is how she did it,' Hawthorne said.

'If you have enough money you can have anybody killed, Inspector,' Delatouche said with a smile.

'But we checked Hilary's bank account,' Hawthorne said. 'She made no large withdrawals recently.'

'She didn't have to,' the accountant explained. 'Keith's political campaign fund took care of that. We had millions of pounds in untraceable accounts. You would never have found it.'

'Let me make sure that I understand you completely,' Hawthorne said. 'Are you telling me that you paid for an assassin to kill Keith?'

'No,' Delatouche said. 'It wasn't me. Hilary paid for the killing.'

'But you gave her Keith's money, didn't you?'

'I did intend to,' Delatouche admitted. 'But I never did. When the murder took place, the money was still in an off-shore account. It's still there now.'

'Hilary is not the kind of person who mingles with contract killers, is she?'

'Nor am I,' Delatouche exclaimed. 'But Keith was. All we did was to ask one of Keith's friends for help.'

'Who did you ask?'

'His name is Brydale. I don't know what happened next. That's the truth,' Delatouche insisted. 'The next thing I knew, Keith was dead.'

CHAPTER 49

At three o'clock in the morning Hawthorne decided that it wasn't worth going home. He drew the blinds in his office and settled on the floor. Dalgliesh stretched between two chairs in the canteen on the far side of the hall.

Two and a half hours later Hawthorne woke suddenly and cursed himself, 'I've been blind!' he yelled. 'Blind, stupid and careless! How could I have been so blind?' With only a dim light reaching into his office from the corridor outside, he began frantically to search his desk.

'Are you alright, sir?' his detective sergeant asked him, knocking on the inspector's office door.

'What? Yes. I'm fine,' Hawthorne responded. 'Turn on the light! Where is the brochure?'

Dalgliesh stared at a blinking inspector who was standing on a makeshift bed of clothing in the middle of his room and was surrounded by pieces of paper.

'What brochure?' the sergeant asked.

'Brydale's company, Defence Consultants Limited, have a glossy brochure boasting about their achievements in Colombia. Oh, where the hell is it?' Hawthorne cried.

'I'm sorry, sir. I don't understand,' Dalgliesh admitted.

'The murdered American oil executive! They spelled it out!' Hawthorne told him. 'They spelled it out. The executive's wife and her American solicitors spelled out in enormous detail, to the chief of police in Bogotá, exactly why her husband had been killed. He was the oil company's head of security. Don't you see? Guarding the Cano Limon Pipeline was his responsibility. And he failed. The executive's wife told the Colombian police that her husband had received threatening phone calls from London after the pipeline had been blown up for the thirty seventh time. But it wasn't his fault. I know whose fault it was! I know exactly who should have been guarding that pipeline.'

'Who, sir?'

'Brydale. Brydale should have been guarding it. His company, Defence Consultants Limited, claimed that guarding the Cano Limon Pipeline was their flagship project. Look, it says so in this brochure. But they cocked it up. The dead man's wife explained all this. But the Colombian police wouldn't believe her. To save himself, the executive needed to put the blame squarely where it belonged. He needed to expose Brydale.'

'I understand, sir,' Dalgliesh interrupted. 'If Brydale was so proud of this high profile contract he couldn't allow an executive to ruin it, could he?'

'I think you're right, Sergeant,' Hawthorne agreed. 'And not only that, but I think he would even have been prepared to commit murder.'

'I've made exactly the same mistake that the police in Colombia made. Just as they did, I assumed that the death in Bogotá was an isolated incident. I couldn't see any connection between the death of this executive and the death of Keith. There was a pattern emerging. I just couldn't see it. How could I have been so blind? Luke did warn me. He told me that his father was in Colombia when the executive died. All of the protagonists are directly linked to one another. It's like a circle of dominoes. Don't you see? In American politics it's common for some of the party leaders to have been chief executives of oil companies. I just didn't see the connection. The dead executive worked for the same corporation that Ambassador Whittler used to be the chief executive of before he became the White House Trade Representative. That same oil giant now has at its head the man whose presidential election campaign Keith Connors was trying to fund when he died.'

'So what you're saying is that there isn't only a single oil death directly linked to Keith Connors, apart from his own. There are two others!' Dalgleish exclaimed.

'This has all happened before! The ambassador and the oil executive have both been murdered and both of the dead men employed Brydale to guard their oil assets.'

'So Brydale must have been in Colombia at the same time as Keith?' Dalgliesh concluded.

'Of course not,' the inspector explained. 'A man like Brydale doesn't get his hands dirty. He is far too clever for that. He would send somebody like Vincent Hanner.'

'And he was in Colombia. Look, it says so in his passport,' Dalgliesh exclaimed, waving a sealed plastic bag containing Vincent Hanner's passport in front of the inspector's face.'

The detective opened his desk drawer and removed a number of gruesome images. Then taking a fingerprint record and a magnifying glass he made a calculation.

'I'm no fingerprint officer,' he admitted. 'But these two sets of prints look similar to me. The bloodstained prints from the Colombian crime scene have already been enlarged.' Hawthorne continued. 'Ask our scenes of crimes officers to compare those fingerprints with Vincent Hanner's and come straight back to me with their results. Don't forget to check Vincent Hanner's bank account. I bet he received two large payments, one immediately after each murder. Hurry please.'

CHAPTER 50

Vincent Hanner was woken by the sound of Hawthorne sliding open the wicket in his cell door. He propped himself on one elbow, while rubbing the sleep from his eyes with the back of his free wrist.

'I've got some photographs to show you,' the detective said. 'Do you want a cup of tea?'

'Yeah, alright,' the prisoner said. 'How long are you going to keep me in here for anyway? I want bail.'

'Can you come outside?' Hawthorne said, allowing a uniformed officer to open Vincent's cell door. 'We'll talk about your bail later. But first there's something I want to show you.'

Vincent Hanner followed the inspector down the corridor and into interview room one, where Sergeant Dalgliesh was sitting next to a familiar tape recorder. The prisoner looked first at Dalgliesh and then at Hawthorne. He then crossed the floor slowly and sat opposite the sergeant.

'I want you to think carefully,' the inspector warned him. 'Think about it before you answer. Can you explain these?' He laid a series of photographs on the interview room table. Each one showed the same mutilated body, but each picture had been taken from a different angle.'

Vincent Hanner looked at the images. He didn't blink. In fact, he hardly reacted at all.

'It's some bloke,' he concluded. 'And he's dead.'

'Ten out of ten for observation,' Dalgliesh remarked. 'Would you happen to know which bloke?'

Hanner smiled and picked one of the pictures up. 'Am I supposed to know him?' he said. 'I don't know this bloke.'

'You should do,' Dalgliesh replied. 'You killed him!'

Vincent Hanner smiled again.

'Where's that cup of tea?' he said. 'I killed him? Is this supposed to be some kind of a joke?'

The detectives covered the table with more photographs, this time showing a courtyard outside the victim's hotel room, a page from

Vincent's own passport, one of his bank statements and some bloody fingerprints.'

'We know everything,' Hawthorne said. 'There's only one thing we can't understand. Why didn't you wear gloves? Did you take them off, or did you, correctly, just think that the Colombians wouldn't know whose fingerprints they were?'

'Is that the bloke from Bogotá!' Hanner exclaimed. 'The American bloke. I thought you were having me on for a minute. I'd forgotten all about him. That was an accident. I went to get some plans from his room, the same as the ones we took from Connors. He surprised me while I was looking through his suitcase. We fought and I stabbed him. If he hadn't disturbed me, he wouldn't have died. I never intended to kill anyone.'

'What interest have you got in engineering drawings?' Dalgliesh asked. 'You're not an engineer.'

'I didn't say I was interested in them, did I?' Hanner retorted. 'I just said I went to get them. That's all. If someone wants to pay me fifteen thousand pounds to get some plans, I'll get them the plans. I don't ask what they're for, do I? What do I care what they're for?'

'Are you asking us to believe that someone really paid you that much money just to steal some drawings?' Hawthorne asked.

'I'm not asking you to believe anything,' Hanner replied. 'You can believe whatever you want. I beat the boy up. I killed the bloke in Colombia. It wasn't supposed to happen like that, but what's done is done. I don't deny any of it. You know that it wasn't me who broke your nose. I wouldn't have told you who did break it. I will always protect my comrades with my life. I'm a soldier, it's what we do: It's part of our honour code. A man like you couldn't understand that. Only, we had that argument, didn't we? And it just slipped out. So I guess you know who did that. It wasn't me.'

'If you co-operate with us we should be able to keep you out of a Colombian gaol,' Hawthorne said. 'I don't know if you have any idea what they're like, but I know I'd rather die than be put in one. You'd be doing a life sentence. I know you're abiding by an honour code and refusing to divulge information on your friends. But let me tell you something. Do you think any of your friends would do a life sentence in a Colombian gaol to protect you? And even if they tried, how long do you think it would take the gaolers out there to beat the information, that investigators are asking for, out of them? They don't have the European Convention On Human Rights out there, you know. Think about it. You've got an opportunity here. If I was you, I'd take it,' the detective said.

CHAPTER 51

From their alcove in the rock face, above the gentle, sandy ridge, Tibra and Hilary watched a dust cloud on the horizon growing larger as it approached. Even from that distance they could see occasional, silver flashes emanating from the centre of the yellow swirl. By the time Hilary realised the approaching, white dot was a Toyota Land Cruiser, travelling at great speed, Tibra had already returned to the fire and was packing away their things. Three veiled boys, yelling and gesticulating, jumped from the back of the moving vehicle. Its driver and one of his passengers wore blue turbans, another wore black, and the last, who had European features, wore jeans and a cheese-cloth shirt.

It was he, who asked the old man in French, 'is this the woman?' The tanned, athletic stranger clambered up the slope, brushing his dark, curly hair out of his eyes and holding a telephone outstretched in her direction as he did so.

'You, telephone,' he said in broken English. 'your, fils, er, boy, he sick.' He paused and then added, 'very bad,' and thrust the phone towards her.

In a blur, which encompassed all of the numbers, she dialled Andall Road General Hospital, Luke's university bed-sit, her own house and Keith's house. She didn't recognise Monique's voice on the answering service, but the message that she and Luke were out, was plain enough.

'The phone,' she said, in French, without thinking, 'can I keep it, to use later?'

The turban-clad passenger, standing between the fire and the rear of the Toyota, clearly spoke both French and the Tuareg language. He relayed her request to the driver.

While they disagreed amongst themselves, both inside and outside the vehicle, the old man leaned towards the fire and said gently, 'keep it as long as you need it. It belongs to the oil company which covers many miles of desert between here and the road. They won't miss it.'

'Who are these men?' she asked, 'and how did they know about my son?'

'The driver, he is my wife's nephew. The others are oil workers. Tibra told us who you were several days ago, and the BBC World Service has carried messages about your son for nearly a week.'

'Where are we and where are we going?' she asked and before he answered, she added more to herself than her companion, 'if only I'd known you spoke French!'

'Now,' he replied, pushing a tamarisk twig through the sand at his feet, 'we are in Algeria. You came across the border a few miles from here, just outside Ghadames. The town behind us is called Ohanet. It's possible to get to the largest Tuareg town of Tamanrasset from here, but it's many miles away. There are only two roads which lead that way, one through the Arak Gorge and the other through the gorge at Amguid, both are manned by military checkpoints. There is another way though, through the crevices in the mountains. The way is not known to many, it's used only by bandits and smugglers. We're taking that route. You'll be safe there.'

She watched him making tea and gestured towards the phone.

'I need to speak to my son,' she said, 'I should go to him. How do the oil workers reach this place?'

The old man smiled, 'that's easy,' he said, softly, 'there's an airport in the desert on the far side of the town.'

The sound of her son's voice surprised her.

'Are you hurt?' she blurted,

'I'm fine,' he replied, 'where are you? And when are you coming home?'

'Luke,' Hilary responded, more urgently this time, 'they told me you were ill. What happened?'

'I'm sorry, Mum, I'm not following you,' her son complained slowly, 'who told you that?'

'I'm in the desert and they told me that the BBC World Service had a report that you were seriously ill in hospital. But the hospital there had no record of you. I've been so worried.'

'Hey, Mum,' Luke continued, 'your friend Major Carter has phoned from Paris. He told me to tell you he's got the missing part of the puzzle, whatever that means, and he said to tell you that what you said in the harbour was right. I didn't understand that part of the message, but he made me write it down. When are you coming home,

Mum? He said stay away from the embassy, whatever you do, don't go anywhere near it. He told me to ask you to call him.'

'I'll be home soon,' she whispered, 'Luke, I love you.' Hilary climbed into the truck and took the crumpled piece of paper from the breast pocket of her torn blouse. She didn't know if the major had betrayed her in Tripoli, or if anyone had, for that matter. She wouldn't tell him where she was, she wasn't completely sure of that in any case. She dialled quickly and recognised the major's voice.

'Carter, it's me, Hilary,' she began, awkwardly, 'My son Luke told me you have some important news.'

'Where have you been?' the major hissed, 'I've been waiting for you to contact me for several days.'

'I hardly know myself, for God's sake!' she replied. 'What's the news?'

'The American who flew you out of the country after Keith was killed, he betrayed you to the Libyan police,' Carter said.

'How do I know that it was he who did it?' Hilary countered. 'If I asked him, I'm sure he would say it was you.'

'Look, someone betrayed you. I've told you who it was. I can't persuade you of my innocence. There isn't time,' Major Carter insisted. 'The French police are outside my hotel now, so I haven't got long. They'll be knocking the door down any minute. If you want to know why you were betrayed ask a man called Stuart Brydale what the Expendability Doctrine is. The Texan who flew you to France in his helicopter is its guardian and Keith was its author and creator. Find out what the Expendability Doctrine is and you'll have all the other answers that you need.'

'Who do I ask?' Hilary protested.

'Start with Simon Hawthorne. You already know him and he knows Brydale. The rest will fall into place from there. Don't go to the embassy. I've said it before and I'll say it one last time. It's not safe. Brydale has his own fuel supply and helicopter. He stores them in the same place that the Texan pilot used. Get Hawthorne to retrieve you himself. I don't care how he does it. Don't trust anyone else and I mean no-one.'

'I've got to go. I've got enough power left to make one last call,' she said. 'I've got to thank you. I haven't done that. Will I see you in England?'

CHAPTER 52

'Stebson, the telephone engineer, says he's got another message from Major Carter on Luke's telephone, sir. The French police have responded to your Interpol alert. The Major was travelling on his own passport. They've pinned him down in Paris. What do you want them to do?' Dalgliesh asked Hawthorne.

'How did he get to Paris?' the detective replied.

'Flights between Paris and Tripoli have never been suspended,' Dalgliesh explained. 'Stebson wants to know what to tell them. What should I tell him, sir?'

'Tell them to wait!' Hawthorne shouted, grabbing his coat. 'What the hell is Carter doing? He knows we're tracking him. After the cock-up I made with the Swiss police he can't be in any doubt about that.'

'It sounds bad, sir,' Dalgliesh explained as the two men hurried into Andall Road. 'Major Carter told Luke there has been some civil unrest in Tripoli and gunfire has been heard coming from the north side of the city for several days.'

'Gunfire?' the inspector replied. 'What kind of gunfire?'

'I don't know,' the sergeant admitted. 'I'm just telling you what he told me.' Hawthorne was out of breath when he reached Luke's house.

'What's happening?' he said 'Where is he?'

'Two agents from the Direction de la Surveillance du Territoire followed Major Carter to a hotel in the Latin Quarter. The DST and the local Paris police are now sitting in the street outside, waiting for instructions.'

'What calls has he made?' Hawthorne snapped. 'Who is he talking to?'

'One call to Luke and two to Defence Intelligence Headquarters at Chicksands in Bedfordshire. He's not making any attempt to disguise his behaviour. He could lose the French Secret Service easily enough if he wanted to. That's what he's trained to do. And why doesn't he use a phone we can't trace? He's making this too easy. I don't like it.

Of course it might be a ploy to divert our attention away from something else,' Stebson responded.

'Why don't you ask him?' Dalgliesh said.

Both Stebson and Hawthorne stared at him.

'What do you mean?' Hawthorne challenged.

'If he's acting as openly as you say he is then perhaps he wants to be approached. Why didn't he contact the Police Nationale in Paris of his own accord if that's the case? But anyway, why not knock on his door and ask him what he's up to. What harm can it do?'

'He knows the DST are watching him. He could be laying a trap for them, sir,' Stebson cautioned. 'This could be a blind.'

Hawthorne stayed quiet. He rubbed his eyes and took a deep breath. Then he took another and released it slowly. He rubbed his eyes again.

'OK,' he said. 'Tell them to knock on the door.'

'The French Secret Service have gone in,' Stebson reported. 'Hold on.'

The landline in Luke's house rang and Stebson answered it.

'Oh,' the telephone engineer said. 'I've got a Colonel Montaigne on the phone from Paris. He says that he wants to speak to you.'

'Hello?' Hawthorne said. 'Yes, this is he. No, don't arrest him. Just speak to him, I said.'

'I can put the phone on a speaker,' Stebson offered. Hawthorne nodded. There was a pause and then Hawthorne continued.

'Major Carter? Major, is that you? What the hell is going on over there? Why did you run off in Geneva? You've caused us no end of trouble.'

'I'm sorry about that,' Major Carter said. 'I had to get to Hilary before anyone else did. You were about to mess that up. She'll contact you to give herself up in a minute. She already knows that she will go to prison for what she's done. And she's prepared to turn herself in. Fly out and get her immediately. Don't wait and don't, whatever you do, contact the Head of Libyan State Security, Moussa Al Ghazal. He imprisoned her in the first place. It is his security force, together with the army, which has been massacring the inmates at her gaol for the last two days. Listen,' he continued. 'Have you arrested Brydale yet?'

'No,' Hawthorne admitted. 'Why do you ask?'

'I thought not,' Major Carter observed. At the back of Andall airfield you'll find a maintenance area. It has two aircraft fuel tanks in it. There should be an AS355 twin- engined Squirrel helicopter there too. It's one of a pair. Mine is one of the names that you'll find on their lease agreements, but never mind that now. If you find the aircraft one of your own police force pilots can take you to Hilary. If you don't, then Brydale has already taken it. In either case use the fuel. You need to get to Hilary before he does. It's her only chance.'

'Why are you telling me this?' Hawthorne asked.

'Because it's the only way that I can salvage the last remnants of my honour. Remember, Inspector, I'm a solider. This is the last decent thing I can do. It's my fault that Hilary got involved in this. I needed to have Keith Connors killed and Brydale sent Vincent Hanner to deal with it. But I didn't know that Brydale had already been approached to do the same thing by Delatouche until Hilary told me. It's clear to me now that Brydale's plan was to kill Keith Connors and blame it on Hilary.'

'So Brydale got paid twice for carrying out Keith's murder.' Hawthorne concluded. 'But why would you want him dead? What possible threat was Keith Connors to you, Major? You didn't even know him.'

'I guard Keith's work,' Major Carter explained. 'The consortium of oil companies which employs me relied on his brainchild, the Expendability Doctrine, to guarantee their profitability. It fell to me to protect it using any means necessary. To understand my reasons you need to read the doctrine. Dr Simmons can give you a copy. My task is to guard it, his task is to ensure the doctrine is complied with.'

'I need you to come back to England and testify in court.'

'I'm not your concern, Inspector. Hilary is. Brydale will have already sent somebody to kill her. You need to get to her before he does. I realise my mistake. There is only one honourable thing that I can do.'

The French Colonel shouted: 'Oh, non! Mon Dieu! Arrêtez vous. Arrêtez vous!'

A loud retort sounded. Then there was silence.

Colonel Montaigne picked up the phone.

'Monsieur Hawthorne,' he said, 'le Chef de Bataillon, il est mort. He is dead. He puts a pistol in his mouth and voilá il est mort.'

Hawthorne's right ear canal was filled with a painful buzzing. At first he neither said nor did anything. He simply stood dazed and rooted to the spot.

'Do you still want it on a speaker?' Stebson asked.

'What?' Hawthorne replied.

'Leave him alone,' Dalgliesh advised. 'Here, let me take the phone.'

'The guy's shot himself!' Stebson exclaimed.

'I know,' Dalgliesh admitted. 'Pull that chair over here. Would you?'

Sergeant Dalgliesh was handing Inspector Hawthorne a glass of water when the inspector spoke, at last.

'Then I guess it's over,' he said.

'What is, sir?' Sergeant Dalgliesh replied. 'I don't understand. What's over?'

'Come, I'll show you,' Hawthorne explained. 'Without Major Carter the whole cabal has no-one at its head. It's over. It's finished. Hilary Connors can come home now. There's simply no-one left to threaten her, Luke, or anyone else. They're all gone, Sergeant. With the Major dead that's it. There's no-one left.'

CHAPTER 53

There were two groups of armed policemen on Andall Airstrip when Hawthorne and Dalgliesh arrived. The door of Brydale's wooden hut was open and all of his possessions had been scattered around.

'There's no sign of him,' an armed policeman said. 'We've looked in the maintenance area. The helicopter and the fuel are still there, but he's not.'

'Bring the sniffer dogs from Operation Extract,' Hawthorne said. 'He's here somewhere. Trust me. I can feel it.'

Hawthorne flicked the open door of Brydale's hut.

'Who opened this door?' he said. 'I mean who unlocked it?'

The armed officer Hawthorne was speaking to looked surprised.

'I don't know who unlocked it, sir,' he replied. 'Does it matter?'

'If the man you're looking for is the only person with a key, I'd imagine that it does matter, yes, Sergeant!' Hawthorne snapped. 'How was the door when you arrived? Was it open or closed?'

'Just like that,' the firearms officer protested. 'We haven't touched it. In fact, we haven't touched anything, sir, nothing at all.'

Hawthorne raised an index finger to his lips.

'Alright, Timothy, you can come down now,' he called out.

For several seconds nobody moved.

'I said you can come down!' Hawthorne snapped irritably.

The two men could hear fabric scraping on a wooden surface above their heads. The armed policeman raised his gun. A second later the soles of a pair of army boots dangled down towards them. The boots were followed by a face, and several drops of blood.

Brydale hadn't managed to dress himself properly. He had a bloodstained, khaki t-shirt on, camouflaged trousers, and a military, knitted cap. Half of his face was covered in grease-paint and the other half was clean.

'Having trouble with our makeup, are we?' Hawthorne enquired, dryly.

The police marksman wasn't smiling though. His machine pistol was trained on Brydale's forehead. And his look of concentration told both Hawthorne and Timothy Brydale what was clearly on his mind.

'You'd better come down, before somebody gets hurt,' Hawthorne advised. 'Easy, keep your hands where we can see them. Just come down smoothly and slowly. Take your time.'

'I need to put my hands inside the edge to spring off from,' Brydale explained.

The police marksman shook his head.

'Keep your hands where I can see them, all the time,' he ordered. 'If you move them, I'll shoot you. Got it?'

Brydale gulped.

'OK, I've got it,' he replied. 'That's pretty clear.'

'Jacket floor! You floor, now!' the marksman bellowed. 'Now, now, now!'

'OK, keep your hair on,' Brydale quipped. 'If you've got to shoot me, I guess that's fair enough. But there's no need to be rude.'

Timothy Brydale jumped down to the ground. He staggered upon landing, but righted himself soon enough. A bloody hand-print remained on his wall, marking the spot on which he'd stumbled. At that moment Hawthorne was unceremoniously catapulted to one side by four armed men. Yelling orders, of all kinds, at the tops of their voices, these newcomers wrestled Brydale to the floor, wrenching his arms behind his back in the process.

'We need to secure the area, sir,' an armed man told Hawthorne. 'Would you mind waiting outside?'

Simon watched the men pouncing on Timothy's back, and he bit his lower lip. 'Well, be careful with him,' he advised. 'I need to ask him some important questions.'

Dalgliesh was crossing a strip of grass between Brydale's office and his aircraft hangar.

'There are aircraft ground crews available to check this helicopter, sir,' Sergeant Dalgliesh said. 'But wouldn't you rather use a police aircraft? I would.'

'No. I'll use this one,' Hawthorne replied, walking around the blue and white, six-seater Eurocopter. 'You don't have to come if you don't want to.'

'Here comes Jarvis,' Dalgliesh remarked.

Some distance from the detectives their rotund superintendent sat conversing with several policemen. To Jarvis' right Chief Superintendent Trent stood. Both men broke from their conversation and crossed the landing strip to where Dalgliesh and Hawthorne were.

'Well,' Jarvis said. 'Do you know who killed Keith Connors yet or not?'

'Yes, sir, I do,' Hawthorne replied. 'In a manner of speaking, he killed himself.'

'For Christ's sake, man, make sense!' Superintendent Jarvis protested. 'How can you possibly assassinate yourself?'

'Vincent Hanner pulled the trigger. He'll admit to it too, in exactly the same way as he has done for the other murders. He was employed by Brydale, and Brydale was hired by a consortium of oil companies to do security work everywhere in the world. Major Carter was part of that consortium. It was he who was ultimately responsible for their actions. Major Carter guided Brydale. Everything that Brydale and his men did, had to be approved by Carter. The Major also had a henchman, a vulgar Texan, renowned for his lack of dress sense. With an affable manner, this Texan could make acquaintances quickly and befriend Carter's targets speedily. He was also not recognised outside America. It was he who attacked Luke, and he also flew Hilary Connors out of the country after her husband's murder. In recent years though, Brydale and his men didn't guard oilfields, pipelines and the like. Instead they were employed to guard intellectual property rights for the oil giants, but intellectual property of a type you've never seen. Their job was to guard a financial strategy called The Expendability Doctrine. It's basically an oil and gas consumption model upon which the entire US economy depends. The US Energy Committee employs a working group to estimate how much oil the US economy needs each year. Energy planners like Doctor Simmons then calculate how best to get that oil. The way the model works is this: Some people, for example those who live too close to rivers near oil refineries, or those who protest about their local habitat being destroyed, are expendable. The oil must be drilled and the people must be silenced or moved by whatever means necessary. None of this is new, but Keith Connors revolutionised the hitherto vague notion of oil industry security. He calculated how many lives need to be sacrificed to meet the US annual oil target. His model predicts how many US soldiers will die acquiring new oilfields. Planners suppress the military death figure by hiring mercenaries to die instead of regular soldiers. The total number of civilian deaths necessary to subjugate a target area is likewise calculated.

Feeding the value of human life into an economic forecast isn't new, by the way, the airline industry does it all the time in cost-benefit analysis. Ambassador Whittler was one of the first people to see Keith's finished model. He was profoundly affected by it. The mistake Whittler made wasn't that he refused to believe this aggressive concept, far from it. The mistake he made was that he believed in it too much. But he completely misunderstood the consortium's reason for inventing the plan. The Expendability Doctrine is framed in terms of territories, security of supply, and strategic gains. It only used that language because military planners and conservative American politicians have always spoken like that. But that's not its real purpose. Put simply: It's a sales document. That's all it was ever supposed to be. The plan was really only ever about profit. It was a business model, nothing more. What Ambassador Whittler did was to take the business plan, and turn it into a political mantra. By doing that, and embracing a man with a reputation like Keith's, he promised to discredit the doctrine and undo all the hard work that had gone into creating and protecting it. The Expendability Doctrine had become a victim of its own success. And Ambassador Whittler, its greatest exponent, had become its greatest liability. But you see, that's where the plan comes into its own, even its architect and its most powerful adherent are expendable. That's its beauty.'

Patrick Mackeown

The Cardinal's Blood

A truly global financial scandal
encompassing the Vatican Bank, the
death of a Milanese Banker, and the
abduction of a British financier, Daniel
Vaughn's, wife and child.

In June of 1982, in the midst of an Italian financial crisis of epic
proportions, the Vatican's most powerful financial advisor, Roberto
Calvi, is found hanging by the neck beneath Blackfriars Bridge in
London. Subsequent autopsies and investigations prove fruitless.
Nevertheless, the ensuing pattern of deaths and disappearances is
murderous in the extreme.

In order to rescue Daniel's family, the narrative races on a white-
knuckle ride across Europe, from the Banks of the Thames, to the
Trastevere, at the ancient heart of Rome.

In an exotic blend of gripping fiction and genuine, historical fact The
Cardinal's Blood tells a story of worldwide fascination.

Published by BookScape in the following formats:

ISBN 978-0-9554328-3-5 Paperback
ISBN 978-0-9554328-4-2 eBook (Adobe Reader)
ISBN 978-0-9554328-5-9 eBook (Mobipocket)

Patrick Mackeown

Midwinter's Children

Patrick Mackeown has written two successful thrillers, and is currently working on his third, Midwinter's Children.

For a list of current and forthcoming titles visit ww.bookscape.co.uk

Printed in the United Kingdom
by Lightning Source UK Ltd.
115542UKS00001B/208-243